A Walk
in the Park

Grace Casselman

Napoleon

Cover art: James Bentley

Published by Napoleon Publishing/RendezVous Press
Toronto, Ontario, Canada

Le Conseil des Arts du Canada | The Canada Council for the Arts
DEPUIS 1957 | SINCE 1957

Napoleon Publishing acknowledges the support of the Canada Council for our publishing program

Printed in Canada

09 08 07 06 05   5 4 3 2 1

Library and Archives Canada Cataloguing in Publication

Casselman, Grace, date-
    A walk in the park / Grace Casselman.

ISBN 1-894917-19-7

    I. Title.

PS8555.A7797W34 2005   jC813'.6
C2004-907039-8

With love to my very dear sisters, Ruth and Sara;
(also Sara and Ruth—you know why).

And to my "Little Sister", Michelle.

The Canadian prairies seem to go on forever.

In every direction, the wheat fields are rolled out flat, disappearing into the sky at the distant horizon.

And that sky is big; actually enormous; stretched over the dome of the whole world like a magnificent blue canvas covered liberally with rolling white clouds.

The overloaded moving truck has gone on ahead.

In the car, Terra and her parents ride silently on the very straight road cut through those fields—each kilometre looking remarkably like the one gone past, and the one yet to come.

There are no other cars on the road. Terra is suddenly gripped by the panicked thought that they are the only ones left alive in the universe; rolling on this unending treadmill of prairie.

But no, Calgary is yet to come, surely. And Terra's new neighbourhood—Inglewood.

one

It was a bleak, grey day in Inglewood. In this dry climate, a really rainy day was rare—but nonetheless, a rainy day had come, and with gusto.

The raindrops splashed enthusiastically against the windshield, eager to soak any hapless victim who might dare to step outside. The car ploughed through an enormous puddle of water and came to rest against the curb—which sadly was a considerable distance from the steps up to the school, a large sandstone structure labelled Inglewood Junior High.

Her mom frowned and fussed. "I wish I could get you closer, Terra. Are you sure you don't want me to come in with you?" Her usually cheerful face was crunched up into an expression of concern. She peered out the window at the rain clouds.

"Definitely not!" In her nervousness, Terra Michelle Morrison spoke too loudly.

Realizing her mom looked a little hurt, Terra sighed. But after all, bringing her mother along on the first day of school would really not help her chances of making a decent first impression. "I can handle it, Mom," she said, in a conciliatory tone. She fiddled with the buttons on her blouse. Maybe she should have worn a T-shirt.

"Should I write you a note saying it's my fault you're late on your first day of school?" her mother asked, turning up the windshield wipers. "But we did have to wait around for the renovator to arrive. You'll meet him later. It was such a rush this morning. You want a note?"

"No, no, it's okay," Terra said, grasping the door handle. She knew she'd better get going, before her mom changed her mind and decided to come in after all.

"I wish you'd worn your boots, Terra. Your feet are going to get wet."

"Mom, really. I'll be okay. Don't worry."

If her mother had had her way, Terra would have arrived at the new school clad in the bright yellow rain slicker and boots that made her look like an overgrown duck. Instead, she'd just look like a drowned rat.

"Isn't Calgary supposed to have a dry climate?" she muttered to herself.

Taking a deep breath, she turned the handle and jumped out into the rain. "Bye, Mom!" she shouted, then slammed the door and began the hundred metre dash. But she ran carefully, watching her footing. She didn't want to start her new school year face-down in the mud.

Just as she reached the bottom step, she heard some thunderous thumps right behind her. "Incoming!" a male voice called out, just before he landed smack in a huge puddle, splashing her ankles with cold water.

"Oh, that's just great."

"Sorry!" he yelled cheerfully. Terra caught a glimpse of a rather mischievous grin, as a tall boy waved and dashed past her up the steps into the school.

Startled, she paused just a moment. However, the water running down her neck reminded her to get moving.

She glanced back at her mother, who was waiting in the car—her neck craned anxiously as her hand frantically waved goodbye, as if the extra energy expended would be transferred into some sort of good luck.

With a forced smile, Terra waved back dutifully, then yanked open the heavy metal door leading into the school.

The hallway in front of her was completely empty. Pausing, she took a moment to wring out the ends of her very wet hair. Then she deliberately squished her running shoes on the floor. "Okay, maybe I'm doing a duck impression after all," she thought to herself, grinning ruefully.

She heard a sound behind her and turned around quickly. Three perfectly coiffed girls stood in the hallway, staring at her, rather as one might look at an alien. Or at a large duck in the middle of a school hallway.

"Um," Terra began. She thought she might ask them for directions to the school office.

To her surprise and discomfort, the girls all started to giggle. With a toss of their lovely heads, they set off down the hall.

"I was wondering…" Terra called out, dripping on the floor. The girls giggled louder and disappeared around the corner.

"Oh, this is going to be just great," she muttered and squished two more times, for effect. Or maybe she was stalling for time.

"Excuse me, young lady," said a deep voice behind her. A tall, thin man with small round wire glasses was frowning at her, his gaze alternating between her face and the puddle gathering at her feet.

"Why aren't you in class?" His voice sounded accusing.

"It's my first day," she told him. She attempted a friendly smile.

He appeared to ignore that and raised an eyebrow at her. "Is that an excuse?"

"Um," said Terra. It really was a decent excuse, wasn't it?

"I mean, I need to go to the main office first." She was a bit breathless, unnerved by the frown on this grim man. "But I don't know where it is."

"Ah," he nodded curtly. "This way, then." He turned on his heel and beckoned for her to follow. Terra scampered after him as he strode down the hall. Her wet running shoes made little squishing sounds that seemed to echo through the corridors.

He turned and frowned at her, his bushy eyebrows drawn together. "I'm the vice-principal, Mr. Brenner. I hope you're serious about school. At Inglewood Junior High, we take academics seriously. It's no walk in the park."

She blinked at him. "Okay. Um. Yes…" She could still feel water dripping down the back of her neck. "So…is the office near here?"

With a curt nod, he pointed to a sign marked "Office". "Just in there." With a squeak of his heel on the waxed floor, he disappeared around a corner.

Somebody had taken a pen and written a big "P" on the sign hanging outside the office, so that it now really said "Poffice".

"That doesn't make sense," Terra thought to herself, perplexed. After all, if someone's going to take the trouble to vandalize something, shouldn't the result at least make some sort of sense? What kind of word is poffice?

Terra shook her head then pushed open the heavy door.

*   *   *

"Students, you have a new classmate," said Mr. VanderVelde, a tall bearded man with a kind, earnest expression. "Her name is Terra Morrison. Everyone say hello to her."

A roomful of Grade Nine students stared at her. No one said anything.

That's just great, Terra thought irritably.

She smiled weakly, nodding her still-damp head. She had a queasy feeling in her stomach, and she wished the floor would swallow her up.

"Uh hum." Mr. VanderVelde cleared his throat. "Well, Terra, please take a seat, and we'll get on with today's math lesson." He quickly scribbled basic formulas on the chalkboard, the short piece of chalk squeaking painfully with each stroke.

Terra slid into her seat and looked at the etchings on the desk in front of her, as the other kids alternately stared directly at her or shot covert glances her way, depending on where they were sitting. Terra sighed and started to copy the assignment down as the teacher wrote it on the board.

Bang! She felt a shudder go through her whole desk. Then a few seconds later, Bang! She turned around to see a dark-haired girl behind her leaning back in her chair, nonchalantly swinging her leg and loudly chewing her gum. Every now and then, she'd deliberately smack it for extra effect.

Terra smiled tentatively.

But the girl only smacked her gum and looked away.

Terra sighed again and continued the assignment.

* * *

In the hallway after class, Terra knelt on the floor, trying to arrange her books in her new locker. It smelled strongly of disinfectant, and the hinges squeaked loudly when she opened the door.

Suddenly a large shadow fell over her. She looked up to

see a group of girls standing close around her.

They stared at her, and for a moment, no one said anything.

"Um, hi?" offered Terra tentatively. She squinted up at them, since the sun was bright in the window behind them.

They just looked at her. Finally, a tall, heavy-set blonde girl spoke. "You're new here, right?"

"Yeah."

Terra blinked at them, tried another smile. No response.

"Where'd you get that shirt?"

Terra glanced down at the button-up cotton shirt she was wearing. "I guess my mother bought it for me."

"Oh. Your MOTHER." They all laughed, as if it were uproariously funny. "Hey, Joyce," said one of the girls, "her mother bought it for her."

"Yeah," said Joyce. "I heard."

Everyone stopped laughing.

"Thing is, it's blue."

"What?" asked Terra, stupefied.

"Well, nobody wears blue, unless we allow it."

Terra frowned at them. "You've got to be kidding."

"Oh, no, we're not kidding. If you want to wear blue, you've got to have our permission. Pay us a fee."

"What?" Terra felt like she was in some sort of weird after-school TV special. "That's crazy."

Joyce nodded and smiled. "Yeah, so we're crazy. But if you wear blue again, be prepared to fork over a payment."

Terra opened her mouth, searching for some appropriate retort. But just then, the bell rang, and the girls around her disappeared. Shaken, she dropped her books in her locker and went looking for biology class.

She slid into a seat at a table. The walls of the room were covered with diagrams of the inside of a variety of animals, including a very large frog. There was a poster of a human without skin, showing off the muscles. Terra grimaced. There was a slight chemical scent in the air.

A large plastic skeleton dangled just a few feet from Terra, grinning maniacally at her. She was just considering moving a little further away when a tall boy with wavy brown hair and mischievous eyes burst into the room.

It was the puddle-thumper!

"Hey!" he stopped suddenly and smiled at her. Then he turned and yelled to the room. "I'm going to sit beside the new girl!" He slid into the seat beside her. "How ya doing?"

"Well, fine," Terra replied cautiously.

"You're new at the school, right?" He cocked an eyebrow at her.

"Yes, it's my first day. We just moved here."

Just then vice-principal Brenner, who apparently also taught biology, started to outline the day's lesson, and the class fell silent.

But her seatmate leaned over and stuck out his hand. "I'm Glenn," he said.

"Terra. Hi," she replied, putting out her own hand for a brief, awkward handshake.

Mr. Brenner frowned at them.

But Glenn just grinned. He waited until the teacher resumed writing on the blackboard and leaned over to whisper, "Welcome, Terra."

Dear Diary:

I don't really like my new school. I don't know anybody. Worse yet, there seem to be some strange mean girls. Otherwise, it feels like everyone is either staring at me or ignoring me. I don't know which is worse.

The courses seem okay. I wish gym wasn't mandatory, but I also got to sign up for art and music, so that's not too bad.

I met a cute boy named Glenn, and at least he talked to me.

Mom seems worried that it will be hard for me to make friends in this new place. Is she feeling guilty, or does she think no one would want to be my friend?

I got a letter from my friend Lisa in Ottawa today. She says she misses me. I miss her too.

two

"What a mess," said Terra, tripping over bits of wood and dropsheets as she stepped in the front door of the new house.

"Oh, I'm sure it won't take too long," replied her mother, smoothly stepping over a hammer. "This house just needs some work. But yes, it's too bad it wasn't done before we moved in. In any case, your dad's work is paying for it, so we can't complain too much."

"Yeah, yeah." Terra shook some sawdust off her shoes.

"Of course, he gets to escape to the office all day," said her mom, hanging her coat in the closet. "Just think of me trying to work here, to the sound of sawing and drilling. I can only imagine what the potential clients on the phone think when they hear the background noise!"

Terra's mom was trying to start up a small public relations firm from her home office.

Terra smiled. "Just tell them you're so successful, you're in the middle of an expansion!"

"Good idea!" laughed her mom. "Wanna help me unpack some dishes?"

Terra scrunched up her face, but nodded, following her mother into the kitchen. They chatted a bit but mostly just unwrapped glasses and plates and placed them in the cupboards in their new kitchen. That was kind of fun, actually, because Terra felt like she was making major decisions about where things would go from here on in.

"Oh, we don't need that," said her mom, referring to the blue plastic milkbag container in Terra's hands.

"What? Why not?"

"I was out grocery shopping, and they sell milk in plastic bottles here, not bags. So I guess we won't have any use for that."

Terra frowned. "You're not going to throw it out?"

"Well, the cupboard space is rather limited, I don't really see the point in keeping it."

Terra thought about all the milk she'd drunk out of bags in that holder. It seemed wrong to throw it out, just because it didn't fit in. "I want it."

Her mother looked bemused but nodded. "Sure, dear."

Terra headed for the stairs, clutching her milkbag holder. She heard a strange noise and spun around.

A very large man with a full red beard appeared in the hall, dragging a step-ladder behind him. "Why, hello," he said cheerfully. "Who are you?"

"Terra," she answered, then blurted out, "I live here."

"Well, that's great," he grinned. "I'm Fred. Fred the Fixer, they call me."

She smiled. "Sorta like Bob the Builder?"

"Exactly," laughed Fred. "Just let me get this out of your way," He dragged the ladder out of her path.

"Oh, you're done?" she asked hopefully.

"No, no, just for today. But don't worry, it's going to be great."

"Uh-huh," she replied noncommittally, looking around at the mess. There was a pile of wood in one corner, along with several cans of paint. Another wall was lined with toolboxes.

He smiled at her. "So, what do you think of Inglewood?"

She shrugged. "It's okay."

"Just okay?" he raised an eyebrow. "You make any friends yet?"

She thought briefly of Glenn, but then again, he'd just thrown her a wave as he ran out when the class bell rang. No one else had really talked to her, although she'd felt a lot of eyes following her around.

"Well, don't worry. I'm sure you'll make friends. You're personable, aren't you?" said Fred, wiping his hands on his overalls. "If you're friendly, people will be friendly to you!"

"Yeah, I guess so."

*   *   *

Actually, it wasn't as easy as that.

Joyce and her friends continued to plague her whenever they got a chance.

Terra tried to ignore them. She told herself she wouldn't let herself be cowed by a couple of bullies.

So why, she asked herself, hadn't she worn blue since that strange encounter?

Then again, she only had that one blue shirt, anyhow. No point over-wearing it, right?

To be fair, the other kids at Inglewood Junior High weren't particularly unfriendly, but they seemed to be settled in established groups of friends. A few kids here and there eyed her with apparent interest, but no one approached her. And Terra didn't have the nerve just to sit down with strangers at lunch without being invited.

After several days of solitary lunch hours, Terra thought perhaps things were looking up.

Walking down the hall, she recognized a familiar face. Glenn was leaning against a locker, chatting with three girls. "Hey, Terra," he called, waving her over. "You should meet some friends of mine." He waved idly in the direction of the girls. "This is Kaitlin, and Tracy and Winter. And this is Terra—T-E-R-R-A," he spelled, grinning.

Tracy, a petite dark-haired girl, just nodded. Actually, she didn't look all that friendly.

"Ah, Terra like 'earth' in Latin," said Winter. She was tall and attractive, with curly black hair and dark skin, dressed in bold red and purple stripes. "That's a great name." She smiled warmly at Terra. "Welcome to Inglewood Junior High, girl." She held out her hand.

"Oh," Terra blushed and shook the proffered hand. "Thanks." Then, uncertain what to say, she added: "I was just going to say how much I liked the name Winter."

Winter's smile broadened. "Thanks."

Kaitlin dropped her books loudly in the bottom of the locker. She pulled a large straw hat over her long medium-brown hair. "Hey!" she protested, targeting her grin at Terra. "Doesn't anybody like my name?"

"Don't answer that," interjected Winter. "She's sufficiently self-absorbed as it is!"

"I never!" exclaimed Kaitlin, looking indignant. "What impudent slander!"

"I beg to differ," Winter replied smoothly. "Justifiable commentary, I say."

Then they both burst out laughing.

Terra blinked.

"They do this," Glenn whispered, shrugging. "Just ignore it. We all do."

"Glenn Waters," admonished Kaitlin. "Just because we're

choosing to…" she paused, "…exercise our vocabularies, there's no need to be rude." She shook her head and turned her back on him. "So, where are you from?"

"Oh. Uh, Ottawa."

Winter whistled. "Wow. That's a long way."

"Have you been up the CN Tower?" interjected Tracy.

Terra squinted. "Well, yeah. But you know that's in Toronto, right?"

Tracy shrugged. "It's all in Ontario, isn't it?"

"Well, yeah. But it's a big province."

"That's for sure," said Winter. "But Ottawa's a beautiful city. My family went there a couple of summers ago. We saw the parliament buildings and visited the National Art Gallery. It was great."

Terra nodded, feeling a bit of a pang. "Yeah. I didn't want to leave, but the engineering company my dad works for transferred him here for work."

Kaitlin and Winter smiled at her sympathetically.

Tracy just looked bored. "Calgary's a better city anyway."

"What do you miss most?" asked Kaitlin, curiously.

"Well, I definitely miss my friends. And…I guess the trees?"

"What do you mean? We have trees."

"Yeah…but I'm just not seeing the bush, the forest, that one sees in Ontario. Especially as you move into Northern Ontario, where we used to vacation. Out here, it just seems really…open and bare."

Winter nodded. "It's the prairies…you'll grow to like it. At least, that's what my father says. He grew up in Montreal, and says he never wants to leave Alberta. Hey…we'd better get going, or we're going to be late."

To prove the point, just then the bell rang, and everyone

rushed off to class. Terra hurried past Mr. Brenner, who stood in the hall, frowning at her.

*   *   *

At lunch in the cafeteria, Terra saw the girls, Tracy, Kaitlin and Winter, drop their knapsacks at a table for four. Kaitlin and Winter headed up to the counter to place their orders.

Terra carried her tray over to the table and smiled brightly at Tracy. "Hi, there!"

Tracy nodded briefly, digging in a lunch bag. "Hi."

Terra felt a little flustered. She felt as though the kids at the next table were all staring at her. "Oh, uh, we met earlier today," said Terra. "Glenn introduced us?"

Tracy nodded and shrugged. "Yeah. I remember."

"Well…is it okay if I sit with you guys?"

Tracy's eyes flickered to the empty seat beside her. She looked over her shoulder at the other girls in line, then back at Terra. "Sorry," she said flatly. "They're all saved."

"Oh," said Terra, embarrassed. "Uh, sure…"

Tracy resumed her examination of her lunch, and Terra backed away, almost running into a huge senior carrying an overflowing tray. "Hey, careful, kid," he growled.

Terra fled to the other side of her room and dropped into the first empty seat.

"Aren't you going to ask me if that seat's taken?" a dry voice inquired mildly.

Terra, still flushed, blinked. She took in the long brown hair and the gum chewing. "You're in my math class," she blurted out.

The other girl raised an eyebrow.

Terra swallowed. "I'm sorry, is this seat saved?"

"Naw." She shrugged and smacked her gum.

"Oh. Good. Um, my name's Terra."

"Yeah, I heard that in class."

"So…" Terra ventured. "What's your name?"

The girl paused her chewing. She looked Terra up and down, still with a raised eyebrow.

Suddenly, unexpectedly, she smiled. The effect was dramatic. She looked almost friendly. "Blaine. How d'ya do?"

*　　*　　*

Terra had to step over a small pile of wood to make her way into the kitchen.

"Mom!" she yelled. "This place is a mess!"

"Oh, don't you worry. Before long, everything will be just beautiful," said a deep but mild voice behind her.

Terra shrieked and spun around.

"Oh," she said, with her hand at her throat. "Fred! I didn't know you were still here."

He blinked at her. His red beard was pale, spotted with sawdust. "Just heading out for the evening. Your mom's up in her office."

"So how long is all this going to take?"

"Oh, not long, not long. But then again, it's hard to know." Fred shook his head, almost sorrowfully. He peered at her from under his bushy eyebrows and grinned. "So how's school going?"

"Not so good," Terra frowned and shrugged. "I miss my friends at my old school. The kids at this school don't seem all that nice.'"

"No?" He raised an eyebrow at her. "Well, give them a chance. I'm sure there's got to be somebody you'll like."

"Yeah." She looked at the floor, and then back up at Fred. "But what if they don't like me?"

"Oh," Fred laughed and waved his hand at her. "Don't worry about that! What's not to like?"

"Yeah," she repeated, unconvinced. "What's not to like?"

*　　*　　*

Her father unwittingly echoed the same topic over dinner.

"Hey, Terra…" He pushed some wood aside and took his place at the dining room table. He smiled at his wife and daughter and said the grace.

"Well, Terra, how do you like your new school?"

She shrugged.

Her parents looked at her expectantly.

"Well…it's okay."

"You don't like it, Terra?" her mom asked. Her voice had a worried tone.

Her father paused, mid-bite, waiting for her answer.

"The classes seem okay," she added, "but I don't really know anybody, so it's not all that fun."

"So make some friends," said her father bluntly.

Terra frowned, but her mother interjected. "Jack, you can't just order her to make friends—that's not how it works."

"It wasn't an order," he protested. "Just a suggestion."

"Well, I'm sure she's trying!" Her mom turned an anxious eye in Terra's direction. "You are trying, aren't you, dear?"

Terra sighed.

"Because sometimes you can be kind of grumpy."

"What?" said her dad. "No way. Terra's the friendliest sort there is." He reached over and touched her on the shoulder. "Right, kid?"

"Yeah, yeah," said Terra, squinting at her mom. Grumpy?

"So you're going to make some friends?"

"Yeah, sure."

Her mom watched her worriedly.

"That's my girl," said her dad with an approving nod.

Terra glumly pushed her food around, while her father enthusiastically finished off his plate.

*   *   *

Lisa too tried to be encouraging when she phoned later that evening.

"Oh, you'll make friends at your new school, Terra. Didn't you have lots of friends here?"

"I guess. But we all grew up together."

"Yeah, but that doesn't matter. I'm sure the kids there will think you're just as nice as we do." Lisa had that familiar teasing, cajoling note in her voice.

Terra rolled her eyes. "Yeah, yeah," she said, settling in a big armchair for a prolonged chat-fest.

But it wasn't to be. "Hey, I can't talk long," Lisa said. "I just wanted to say a quick hello. Some of the girls are coming over to work on a biology project."

"Oh," said Terra. She felt a bit of a pang, because she wasn't one of the girls going over to Lisa's.

"We're doing experiments on bean sprouts."

"Yeah, well...I'll see you," said Terra. She hung up the phone, lay on her bed and stared at her ceiling for a long time.

Dear Diary:

   My parents don't understand what they're putting me

through. Basically they just uprooted me, and they expect me to be happy about it.

The kids here aren't very friendly. I tried to talk to a couple of them, but I didn't get very far.

I miss my old friends, especially Lisa. She phoned me tonight and told me the people who bought our old house are painting it pink. Pink! What was wrong with off-white, I'd like to know!

I got an A on today's surprise math quiz. I think the girl behind me might have been trying to copy my answers.

Terra closed her diary and shoved it into her drawer.

Then, on impulse, she dug for the envelope that she kept beneath her underwear and pulled out the two photos. The first showed a young woman with long dark hair and brown eyes, not unlike Terra's own. She turned it over; all that was written on the back was "Donna".

The other photo showed the same woman smiling into the camera, leaning against a pillow, clutching a small baby. "A rather ugly baby, with a pointy head," Terra thought to herself, with a frown.

There was a small crumpled note in the envelope, but Terra didn't open it. She held it in the palm of her hand for a moment, then suddenly shoved everything back in the envelope. Carefully, she slid the envelope back beneath the underwear.

three

Terra could feel her heart pounding against the walls of her chest. She bent over to take a deep breath, just in time to hear Ms. Brown, the gym teacher, bellow: "Keep moving, Terra, you've got to keep your heart rate up."

Terra managed an insincere smile for the teacher and began to run. Finally, she came to the end of the track. Blaine lounged in her gym clothes on the bleachers.

"Hey. You don't have to run?"

"Naw." Blaine loudly smacked her gum. "I've got terrible cramps."

Terra looked at her dubiously. The other girl looked cheerful enough.

Blaine grinned. Then, as if to demonstrate the point, she grabbed her stomach and moaned pathetically.

Terra blinked. "Ah. Does that work?"

Blaine shrugged philosophically. "Sorta. They used to make me run anyhow. So I took it up with the vice-principal." She grinned. "I went crying to his office. He was very uncomfortable... Long story short: now I get gym class off once a month." Blaine took out a little bottle and started painting her nails a bright red.

Ms. Brown frowned at them. "Blaine, are you doing that extra health homework?"

"Yeah, Ms. Brown." Blaine patted the book on the bleacher beside her. "I'm working on it."

The teacher looked like she wanted to say more. Instead she clapped her hands together. "Come on, Terra, one more lap!"

Blaine laughed softly. "See ya."

Terra began running again.

A whistle blew shrilly. "Faster, Terra, faster," urged Ms. Brown.

Terra thought she could hear the sound of laughter behind her.

* * *

The changeroom smelled. But it wasn't so much the sweat and running shoes as the proliferation of perfumes, deodorants, gels and hairsprays that gave the girls' changeroom its distinctive odour.

The sound of the girls' chatter seemed to echo off the high ceiling, doubling its intensity. As the other girls moved out of the changeroom, the sudden silence seemed rather eerie.

Terra stuffed her gym clothes into her bag.

"Hey, there," said a friendly voice.

Terra looked up, pleased. "Hi, Winter."

"How's it going?"

"I'm a bit worn out from running around the track."

Winter sighed dramatically. "Yeah, that's what I've got to look forward to." She discarded her bright purple top for the standard gym jersey. "Too bad we're not in the same class."

"Ms. Brown is kind of tough, isn't she?"

Winter pursed her lips. "Ah, I don't know, she's not so bad." She grinned. "Maybe she likes you. Do you have..." Winter stressed the word, *"potential"*?

Terra laughed self-consciously and shook her head. "I'm not very good at sports."

"Practice makes perfect. Well, sorta." Winter smiled, wiggled into her purple running shoes. "I'd better get going. See ya around, Terra." She waved and headed into the gym.

"Yeah, see you," Terra echoed.

*   *   *

As Terra heaved her books into the bottom of her locker, she was surprised to see Blaine plop down on the floor beside her. "Heya."

"Hi." The other girl seemed to have warmed to her a bit, but Terra wasn't quite sure what to make of her.

"Whatcha doing?"

"Um, just getting ready for home."

"You gotta go there right away?"

"No-o," Terra answered slowly. "Not really. Why?"

Blaine shrugged. "I like to hang out in the park."

"Oh," said Terra uncertainly. A park sounded nice, didn't it?

"Well, uh, can I come?"

"Whatever. I don't care." And Blaine started off down the hall.

What? Terra stared, perplexed. But she quickly grabbed her homework, shut the locker and ran after Blaine.

"Hey look!" Terra pointed to a small brown animal, standing on its back legs, its head tilted curiously. It watched as the girls approached, then suddenly dashed into a hole.

Blaine gave her an odd look. "Uh...yeah? You've never seen a gopher before?"

"Oh, is that what it is? Yeah, I've seen a few of them since we got to Alberta. They're really cute."

"Heh. A lot of people here don't like them very much."

"Really? Why not?"

She shrugged. "They make holes and wreck lawns and gardens... I don't know. I don't care. Didn't you have gophers in—where did you say you were from?"

"Ottawa. I don't think so...we had a lot of groundhogs, though. I haven't seen any here...do you have them?"

Blaine shrugged. "What do they look like?"

"Well, they're bigger and fatter. Sort of rabbit-sized. They get hit by cars a lot, on the highway."

"Oh yeah? Cool," grinned Blaine.

"Blaine!" exclaimed Terra, indignant.

"Oh. Uh...yeah, that's too bad, I mean."

"I think your rabbits are bigger, though."

"Huh?"

"I mean I've seen some big...well, what we'd call jackrabbits, but not bunnies. Don't you have bunnies here?"

Blaine chuckled. "Heh, bunnies."

The two girls tramped through the grass then curled up under a big tree.

Blaine pulled out a bottle of polish and went to work on her nails. She didn't seem to want to talk much, although Terra tried to start up a conversation.

"Have you lived in Inglewood long?"

"Yeah."

"Oh."

Terra tried again. "So...do you like it?"

"Uh...whatever."

Terra nodded. "Oh. Um...I just moved here."

"Yeah, I figured."

Blaine blew on her nails to dry them.

Terra leaned back against the tree, looking around the big park.

A lot of kids hung out in groups under the trees or sat on the benches. A few were reading—schoolbooks or magazines, but most just lounged around talking.

"Hey, Blaine," greeted one tall lanky fellow. "Ya got a light?"

To Terra's surprise, Blaine reached into her jean jacket and flipped a small object in his direction.

"Cool," he said, catching it. He pulled a cigarette out of his pocket and lit it, puffing rapidly. He eyed Terra curiously.

"Hey. Who are you?"

Before Terra could respond, Blaine interjected: "That's Terra, Pete."

Terra nodded to him. She felt a bit uncomfortable. She wasn't really used to being around smokers, and her parents wouldn't be happy about it. Still, hanging out with these strange kids in the park seemed like a bit of an adventure.

Pete held the cigarette out to Terra. "Wanna smoke?"

Terra felt her heart skip a beat. She quickly shook her head.

Pete shrugged and took a long drag on the cigarette. He blew out the smoke then leaned over and kissed Blaine on the mouth.

Terra blinked in surprise, especially when Blaine reached over for the cigarette, inhaling deeply.

Another girl ran up and took the cigarette. "Who's that?" She tilted her head at Terra.

"Terra," answered Pete. "Gimme that smoke, Paula."

Paula tossed her short blonde hair and took another puff on the cigarette before handing it back to Pete. "Hey, Blaine."

"Hey."

"I haven't seen you before," Paula said, almost challengingly.

Terra opened her mouth to reply, but Blaine beat her to it. "She's new."

Paula looked Terra up and down, then shrugged. "Whatever." She walked off.

"Um. I should probably get going."

Pete flicked the butt of the cigarette down and ground it out with his heel. "See ya."

Blaine gave her a half-wave.

Terra waved hesitantly too and started walking towards home. These kids were strange.

To her surprise, she heard a deep voice calling her name. "Terra!"

Glenn ran up behind her. "Hey there! How's it going?"

She gave a nervous laugh. "Okay. You?"

"Good!" He paused. "So, I saw you with those kids. You a smoker?"

"No…no. My parents would freak out. Um…are you?"

"Naw," he shook his head. "Well, not any more."

She wanted to ask more but wasn't sure how to phrase it. "Are you making many friends?"

Terra thought of the kids in the park. "A few."

Glenn nodded. "Those girls I introduced you to—they're cool."

Terra thought of the disastrous encounter with Tracy in the cafeteria. "Yeah, they seemed…nice," she responded lamely.

"So are you heading home?" Glenn gestured ahead of them.

"Yeah, it's just a couple of blocks this way."

"You mind if I walk with you?"

"Sure," Terra stammered, flustered. Quickly, she added: "I mean, sure it's okay. Sure it's okay."

She was still smiling when she walked through her front door into the foyer, but she stopped suddenly when the door banged into a ladder.

"Whoa." Fred climbed laboriously down the ladder with

a bucket of rose-colored paint in his hand. "I'm glad this didn't fall on you."

Terra blinked at him. "Yeah, me too. It's not my colour."

Fred laughed and set the can of paint on the floor. "Hey, that's a good one. Not your colour..."

"Hey, Fred. There's a really pretty bird outside, I was wondering if you know what kind it is."

"Oh, yeah? What does it look like?" Fred walked over to the front entrance window and craned his head, for a sight of the bird.

"It's black and white—it's very striking."

"Black and white? Black and white?!" He drew his eyebrows together, almost ferociously. "A magpie? You think a magpie is a pretty bird?!"

"I guess. You don't like magpies?"

"Not really. They're scavengers, like rats of the air."

"Oh," Terra blinked. "I thought they looked nice."

"Mind you," Fred continued thoughtfully. "Not that we have rats..."

"What?"

"Rats are illegal in Alberta."

Terra laughed, thinking he was joking. "What do you mean?"

"Alberta is a rat-free province."

She frowned. "But rats are everywhere, aren't they?"

"Not in Alberta," said Fred firmly. "I heard they can't get across the mountains."

"But what keeps them from crossing the Saskatchewan border?"

"The rat police."

"What?" Terra giggled.

"I'm serious. There are rat police that patrol border farms, to kill any rats that might cross into the province."

"Um…" Terra squinted at him, to see if he could possibly be kidding. But he looked serious.

"Why?"

"They carry diseases. Eat house foundations…you know, bad stuff."

"I never heard of rats eating foundations in Ontario."

"Well, we keep them out here…with the rat police," Fred added cheerily.

Dear Diary:

I was told today that rats are illegal in Alberta. Do you think that can be true?"

My parents picked PINK for the walls in the front entranceway. I told Mom I hate pink, but she said it's not pink, it's rose. Isn't that the same thing? Dad said just to think of it as slightly reddish off-white, but there's no getting around it—it's pink.

Why do girls get stuck with pukey pink anyhow? What makes pink more feminine than any of the good colours, like forest green or royal blue?

Glenn walked me home today—the first time a boy ever walked me home from school, unless you count Matthew from Grade Four. But then again, he was a really small kid, and I think he saw me as protection from the Grade Five bullies. I wonder who he's walking home with now? Maybe he's grown...?

Did I mention that Glenn is really cute?

I hung out after school today with a girl named Blaine, from my math class. She smokes and seems to have a weird boyfriend, but at least she talks to me, sort of…

four

"So what do you think?" Blaine did a little twirl in front of the store's triple mirror. The jeans outlined her slim shape, then flared a bit at the bottoms.

"They're really nice," said Terra, eyeing a dark purple blouse. Maybe she could talk her mom into a shopping trip one day soon. "Are you going to buy them?"

Blaine frowned, sighed. "I can't really afford them." She brightened. "But I guess I could always return them." She darted back into the changeroom to pull off the jeans.

Terra frowned. "What do you mean?" she called through the door.

"Well, I could wear them out with Pete on Friday, and then return them on Monday. As long as I don't cut off the tags or spill something on them, it shouldn't be a problem."

Terra felt a small twinge in her stomach—a feeling that got more familiar the more she hung out with Blaine.

"But that's not really right..." she started.

"What do you mean?" asked Blaine, popping back out of the changeroom.

"Well, it's sort of like stealing, isn't it?"

Blaine stared at her. "Not really. I mean, the store gets them back, so who's hurt? It's kind of like borrowing stuff for a couple of days."

Terra shook her head, unsure. Her parents definitely wouldn't approve of "borrowing" stuff from the store like that.

Blaine shrugged, but she hung the jeans back on the rack.

"Whatever. I have enough jeans anyway. Come on, let's go see where Paula's at."

They met up with her near the entrance to the mall. She tossed a chocolate bar to each of the girls.

"Hey, thanks," said Terra, opening hers and taking a bite. "It was really nice of you to buy that for me."

Paula snorted. "Yeah, right."

Blaine laughed.

"What's so funny?" Terra frowned.

"Oh, nothing," said Blaine. "Just, if I know Paula, she probably didn't buy them."

"What?" said Terra, her mouth so full of chocolate that it suddenly seemed impossible to swallow. She had that uncomfortable feeling in her stomach again.

"Oh, well," said Blaine, as she bit into her candy. "At least, we're not going to bring them back."

"What?" Terra repeated.

Blaine smiled. "I know how you hate borrowing..."

Terra felt her stomach turn over. "Uh, I gotta go," she said, running back into the mall.

"Where ya going?" protested Blaine.

Terra didn't answer, just ran through the doors, hearing Paula and Blaine's laughter echoing behind her.

Retching, she made it to the toilet just in time.

*   *   *

Terra knew she was definitely going to be sick. She could feel her stomach moving around in unpleasant ways. She folded her arms on the table, put her head down and moaned pitifully. "This is really horrible."

Glenn chuckled. "Oh, it's not so bad. You eat meat, don't you?"

"I don't eat rats!" Terra groaned. She lifted her head and snuck a peek at the large rat that Glenn had already pinned to a specimen board for dissection. The strong-smelling preservatives had turned its white fur slightly yellow, and a swollen grey tongue lolled out of its mouth.

"I was told that rats are illegal in Alberta!"

"Yeah, I heard that too. Schools must import dead ones for dissection."

"This is really horrible," Terra repeated. For once, she couldn't even think about how cute Glenn was, even though he was her lab partner. All she could concentrate on was the horrible fat rat. "I'm going to have nightmares. Actually, I'm going to be sick..." She put her hand on her stomach and tried to take slow, deep breaths.

"Hey, Terra," said Glenn, for once without the teasing tone. "Are you okay? You look kind of funny. Here, why don't I do the cutting? You can do the drawing."

Terra took a deep breath, her head turned away from the smell of the rat. "Okay." She watched as Glenn cut through the top layer of skin and flesh and pinned it back to expose the inner organs.

"You get sick easily?"

"Yeah. My mom says I have a nervous stomach." She stared at the rat and whispered, "Why do they make us do this?"

Glenn tilted his head, considering. "I guess this has more of an impact than just reading it out of books."

Terra peeked at the rat and grimaced.

"I sometimes think we should have to kill our own cows and chickens. We'd probably be less likely to waste meat, don't you think?" he said, poking at the rat with his scalpel.

"Will you please stop talking about food?" Terra hissed.

Glenn grinned. "Sorry. I didn't mean to get philosophical."

"No, no. Philosophy's okay. It's just food I don't want to hear about."

He laughed. "Okay, it's a deal."

Across the table, Kaitlin, holding a rat by its pins, was making it dance. "Heya, Glenn," she hissed, pressing her tongue against her teeth. "Check this out." The rat, with its tongue hanging out of its mouth, seemed to dance an enthusiastic jig. But one of the pins slipped out of Kaitlin's grasp, and the rat went flying, landing in the lap of a red-headed boy named Chuck. He went very pale.

"Hey, Chuck," said Glenn, pushing his board across the table. "Did you know people eat these in some countries?"

In an instant, Chuck's colour turned from white to green. He bolted up and made it to the garbage can just in time. The class burst out in a mixture of gasps, groans and laughter.

Terra felt her own stomach roll. She covered her mouth, willing her breakfast to stay down.

"Hey, Terra. I think you're really pretty," whispered Glenn.

"What?" Terra stared at him, startled.

"You looked like you needed a distraction."

"Oh." She flushed, confused.

"Ah, man," said Glenn. "Sorry about that, Chuck."

Chuck waved his hand at Glenn, his head still stuck in the garbage.

Terra searched for something normal to say. "Um...are there really rat police in Alberta?"

"The Rat Patrol!" exclaimed Kaitlin. "Yeah. I did a project on it once. According to the Alberta government, Alberta's rat control efforts have saved one billion dollars over fifty years."

"Huh," said Terra. "I used to have a friend that had pet rats."

"In Ottawa?"

"Yeah."

"Aw," Kaitlin sighed, peering at her yellowish rat with the grey tongue. "It's too bad they're illegal—they're kind of cute."

Dear Diary

I remember visiting my grandparents on their farm near Ottawa. A rat was outside, off the back kitchen and Grandpa said that was weird behaviour and maybe it was rabid. So my Grandpa and bigger boy cousins went outside and hit it with sticks.

I wasn't allowed to go out. They said I was too small.

But I watched out the window. The rat lay still and bloody on the step for a long time before my cousins took it away.

It gave me a weird feeling.

Glenn told me today he thinks I'm pretty, while we were dissecting rats. Is that a bad sign? Could my first real romance be starting over a dead rat?

I hung out with Blaine and Paula today. They seem to know a lot of people, so that's kind of fun.

Fred is banging in the hallway, building some sort of cupboard, I think. How long are these renovations going to take?

Am I pretty? Was Glenn just trying to stop me from throwing up on him?

five

With a tired sigh, Terra closed her diary and shoved it under her pillow. She lay on her back, cradling her head in her palms, and stared at the ceiling for a while.

There was a tap at the door, and her father poked his head in the room. "Hey Terra. How's it going?"

"Okay."

"Did you have a good day at school?"

Should she answer honestly? Why not? "Well, it wasn't so great. We had to dissect rats in school, and one boy threw up."

Her dad burst out laughing. "Really? So which was worse?"

Terra smiled too, reluctantly. "I dunno. They were both pretty gross. And it's not fair. Lisa told me that at our school in Ottawa, they're growing bean sprouts. Bean sprouts, Dad—and I have to cut up rats!"

"Some people might think you're getting the more exciting opportunity."

"Yeah, who? Some sort of deviant, maybe."

Her father chuckled. "No, really, Terra. Say you want to be a doctor. It would be important for you to understand how our bodies work."

"Dad! We dissected rats, not people!"

"I know...but I guess you'd have to start somewhere, right?"

Terra sighed. "I don't want to be a doctor, anyway. This other girl, Kaitlin, says she might want to be a doctor."

"Hmm. So what do you want to be?"

"Oh, I don't know. I don't have to decide yet, do I?"

Her dad shook his head. "Not at all, I just thought you might have some aspirations to share."

Terra squinted at him. "Well, maybe a psychologist."

"Oh?"

"Yeah. I want to learn why people act the way they do."

Her dad laughed. "Yeah, that would be useful. I bet your mom wishes she'd studied psychology. She's always trying to figure me out!

"By the way, after Fred finishes with the living room renovations and the changes to Mom's office, and maybe some work in the kitchen, he's going to paint the rest of house."

Terra rolled her eyes.

"So, I was thinking you might like to pick the colour for your room."

She shrugged. "I don't care."

"Come on. You must have some thoughts...pink?"

"No!"

He grinned. "See? I knew you cared..."

She sat up and looked at the walls, currently an uninspiring off-white with bits of paint peeling off here and there, exposing the drywall underneath.

"Hey, Dad..?"

"Hmm?"

"How about I paint my own room?"

He hesitated for a moment, then nodded. "That sounds like a great idea. You should be able to paint your own room if you want to. You have to live in it, after all."

She nodded. "So...can I paint it whatever colour I want?"

"Sure. Just tell Fred what colour you need, and he can pick up the paint and supplies for you when he goes to the hardware store."

"Wow, thanks Dad!" Terra stood up and flung her arms around him. "It's going to be great!"

Later, she found Fred working away downstairs and handed him her list. He looked at it for a long time without saying anything. Finally, he pursed his lips and pondered her carefully. "You're sure your dad said this was okay?"

"He said I could paint the room however I wanted."

Fred slipped the paper in the front of his overalls. "All right then. I'm on the case."

Terra grinned. "This is going to be so cool."

* * *

"Wow."

Her dad shook his head. "Wow," he repeated. "Um...wow."

Terra beamed. "Isn't it fun?"

"It's certainly something," her dad agreed. "Has your mother seen it yet?"

"No, she said she'd stay out until I finished, as long as Fred was helping me."

"Ah," said her father. "Well, it's certainly very unique and creative. I can honestly say I don't know anyone else who has a solar system in their bedroom."

Terra had painted her walls a deep blue, except for one wall, which was mostly covered by a bright, glowing sun. From there, the planets radiated outwards—Mercury, Venus, Earth, Mars, Jupiter, Saturn, Uranus, Neptune and Pluto. She had included all the rings and moons, according to the astronomy book she'd borrowed from the school library. She'd left one blue wall otherwise empty for the moment, but she planned to paint some constellations on there when she got a chance.

Just then her mother knocked on the door. "Hey, is it safe to come in yet?"

"Sure." Terra opened the door and gestured to the solar system. "What do you think."

Her mom's eyes got very wide. She blinked several times, then looked again. Then she looked at Terra's father. He just smiled and shrugged back at her.

"Wow," said her mother.

"Yeah, that's what Dad said too."

Then her mother laughed, shaking her head. She gave Terra a little hug. "It's not what I expected, Terra, but it's great. It really is."

Terra smiled too. "Thank you!" She opened the door even wider and leaned out to shout down the hall to Fred: "See! I told you they'd like it!"

*   *   *

"Hey, Terra," said Blaine, walking past her locker after school. "Wanna go to the park?"

"Yeah, sure." Terra awkwardly stuffed her homework into her knapsack and swung it over her shoulder. She hurried to catch up to Blaine.

In the park, a few kids were lounging under a big tree, including Paula and Pete. "Hey, kid," said Pete, squinting at her as he slung an arm around Blaine.

"Hi," said Terra. She dropped her knapsack and sank down on the ground beside Paula. The grass was long and coarse by the tree, and Terra could feel it poking her, even through her jeans.

"How are you?" she asked politely.

Paula stared blankly at her for a long moment. Finally, she tossed her hair over her shoulder and looked away. "Just peachy. You?"

Terra flushed a bit. Did everyone have to have an attitude? "Oh, okay, I guess."

Paula grunted noncommittally. She took a small package out of her pocket and handed it over to Pete.

"Here. I made you guys some brownies." She smiled, rather smugly.

"Hey, cool." He shoved them in his pocket.

It all seemed a bit strange to Terra. "You bake?" she asked Paula.

Paula gave a short dry laugh. "Just special brownies."

Terra wondered if she looked as confused as she felt. Apparently so, because Blaine sighed and leaned over to whisper: "They have hash in them, Terra. Ya know, drugs?"

"Oh," said Terra, rather astonished.

Paula just rolled her eyes.

In the distance, Joyce and her friends appeared, walking in their direction.

Terra stiffened involuntarily.

Paula noticed and eyed her curiously. "Are they giving you a hard time?"

"Oh, well..." Terra hesitated, then nodded. "I guess you could say that."

Paula grunted.

"Hey, Joyce," she called as the girls were about to walk by.

"Yeah?" Joyce looked startled, almost nervous, as she answered Paula.

Paula jerked her head in a "come here" sort of gesture. Joyce moved a couple of steps closer. The other kids watched with interest.

"Hey, Joyce. This is Terra."

"Uh, hey," the tall girl said, her eyes flickering from Terra to Blaine and Pete and back to Paula.

Terra could feel her heart beating uncomfortably fast. "Hi," she whispered. "We've sort of met."

Paula toyed with a stone, pushing it about with the tip of her sneaker. Finally, she glanced up at Joyce. "Did ya know she's a friend of ours?"

Joyce swallowed, shook her head. "No, no. I didn't know."

Paula kicked the stone so that it rolled in Joyce's direction. "Now you do."

Joyce backed away, nodded. "Okay, uh, sorry."

Paula shrugged and turned away from her.

Joyce took a step back and hurriedly rejoined her friends. The group quickly moved on.

Blaine burst out laughing. "Nice one!"

"Joyce is afraid of us," Blaine said to Terra. "Well, especially of Paula."

Paula snorted. "Yeah, whatever."

"Everyone's afraid of Paula," Pete joked.

Paula shot him a nasty look.

No one said anything for a moment.

I'm actually kind of afraid of Paula, Terra thought to herself.

"Um…I didn't know you thought of me as your friend, Paula," she ventured.

Paula just shrugged. "Whatever." She reached into her pocket, pulled out a cigarette and lit it. She took a drag from it and handed it to Blaine and Pete. She lit a second one, and smoked it, blowing out long puffs of smoke. "Here," she said, holding it out Terra.

Terra hesitated. Her heart was beating very fast again.

"You don't have to…" Blaine started, but Paula raised a hand, and Blaine fell silent.

Terra took the cigarette from Paula, careful to hold the glowing end away from herself. She raised it to her mouth and sucked on it. Her mouth filled with a strange, somewhat unpleasant sensation. She coughed.

Pete started laughing.

Terra blushed and raised the cigarette to her mouth again. She felt a bit light-headed. At least this time she didn't cough. She handed the cigarette back to Paula.

Paula smiled at Terra.

Dear Diary:

I smoked a cigarette.

The smoking wasn't great, but it felt kind of exciting. And I'm making friends.

Fred gave me a funny look when I got in; I wonder if my clothes smelled? I put them in the wash though, and nobody else noticed anything.

Plus, Joyce is leaving me alone, which is a big relief.

Lisa is coming to visit this weekend. I'm so excited.

six

"Eeiiiiiiii! Eeeeiiiiii!" The girls shrieked, jumped and hugged each other on the front lawn as the bright red minivan bearing the rest of Lisa's family pulled away.

"I'm so glad to see you!" they both shouted, at exactly the same time. Then they burst out laughing and shrieked again.

Terra's mom pulled back the curtain at the window to make sure no one was being tortured. She waved at the two girls, then turned away from the window.

Lisa, a petite girl with curly blonde hair and big blue eyes, giggled. "It's been so long! I couldn't wait to get here! And I'm so glad to get away from my little brother. On the plane, and then in the car, he wouldn't stop singing: 'It's the song that never ends…' He's driving me crazy with his singing. Actually, yelling is more like it; he's a terrible singer!"

Terra laughed. "I remember! How long can you stay?"

"Just until suppertime—I have to join my family for dinner at my Great-aunt Rose's. My mom says I can't skip the whole family visit! Still, we've got most of the day together. Then tomorrow we're driving up to Edmonton to visit my grandmother."

"It's so great to see you. I missed you so much!"

"Me too!"

Terra led her into the house, past the pile of wood and

debris, where Fred was demolishing (and hopefully eventually refinishing) the entranceway to the living room.

"Hey, Fred," said Terra. "This is Lisa—my best friend in the whole world."

"Wow," said Fred, wiping the sawdust from his hand on his overalls before offering it to Lisa, "then this is certainly an honour."

Lisa blushed a little and shook his hand. "So you're fixing up the place?"

"That's right! I'm Fred the Fixer!"

"Cute," grinned Lisa.

"Thank you, thank you very much," drawled Fred, in his best Elvis imitation.

Terra rolled her eyes and pulled Lisa by her arm up the stairs to her bedroom. The sound of hammering followed them up the stairs.

After Lisa had admired the solar system in Terra's room, the girls sprawled sideways on the bed.

They talked and talked.

Lisa tried to update Terra on the goings-on of all their mutual friends and acquaintances. "…so Dana has a big crush on David, and so do Linda and Tammy. But apparently David really likes Trina."

Terra frowned. "I'm surprised David is so popular. He's nice…but..." she whispered, "isn't he really short?"

Lisa stared at her friend for a moment then laughed. "Oh Terra! He grew! You should see him now."

"Oh." Terra felt out-of-touch with her old classmates.

"And Terry is actually growing a beard—at fourteen; can you believe it? So he looks way older…"

"Huh," said Terra. She got up and paced around her room. It seemed unusually small. "So do you want to go for a walk?"

"Sure." Lisa happily followed Terra towards the front door. Terra paused. "Mom?"

She shouted louder. "Mom!"

"Yes, dear?" Her mother stood upstairs outside her office, peering down over the banister.

"We're going for a walk."

"Well, that's good! Have fun, girls." She disappeared back into her office.

They walked companionably down the block. Lisa was bouncing along the sidewalk, chatting about various kids and happenings in her life.

Terra took her by the front of the school building. They stared up at the imposing sandstone structure. On the weekend, the schoolyard was empty and eerily quiet.

"It's big, isn't it?"

"Yeah," agreed Terra. "It's pretty big."

The girls walked across the street to the park. To Terra's surprise, a group of kids was hanging out there, even though it was a Saturday. "Hey, Terra," waved Blaine.

"Yo," said Paula, eyeing Lisa speculatively.

"Hi!" Terra felt a little better, now that Lisa could see that she'd managed to make some new friends.

"Hello," said Pete, lifting an eyebrow at Lisa. "Who's this? Another new kid?"

"This is my friend Lisa, come to visit from Ottawa."

"Ah. How exciting," Pete said in a bored sort of way.

Lisa blinked at him. "Um, yeah. I guess so." She looked uncertain, especially when Pete and Paula lit up cigarettes.

Terra felt torn. After all, Lisa was her oldest, dearest friend, and she probably wasn't that comfortable with the smoking. Maybe they should just keep on going.

Then again, these were her new friends, and she wanted to

hang out with them too. Plus, wouldn't it be nice if her old friend and her new friends could get to know each other?

She sat down on the grass, and Lisa squatted down beside her.

"So you know Terra from way back when or what?" asked Blaine.

Lisa nodded. "Yes, we've been best friends since kindergarten. I was terrified, but Terra took me by the hand and showed me how to use the finger-painting station."

Blaine smiled tolerantly.

But Paula just rolled her eyes.

Pete handed his cigarette to Blaine then lit another one. He offered the package to Terra. She could feel Lisa's eyes on her and hesitated. "Well?" said Pete, impatiently.

"Yeah, thanks." Striving to look nonchalant, Terra took a cigarette and lit it, using Pete's lighter. She tossed her hair and glanced over at Lisa, who was just staring at her.

"Ya don't smoke?" Paula nonchalantly blew out a long stream of smoke.

Lisa shook her head. "It's not good for you."

Pete, Paula and Blaine laughed. Even Terra smiled, although she wasn't sure why.

Paula snorted. "Nobody lives forever."

"No, but…" Lisa looked down at her hands folded in her lap.

Pete mumbled something under his breath. Terra couldn't quite make it out, but she was afraid it wasn't complimentary. Blaine elbowed him in the ribs.

"Cut it out!" he murmured, then fell silent.

Lisa looked like she was going to cry.

Terra felt as though she was going to throw up, but then again, that could have been because of the cigarette. Trying to appear nonchalant, she handed the remainder back to Pete. "Well, we'd better go."

Lisa leapt up, almost eagerly. "Bye," she said to the others.

"Nice to meet you, Lisa," nodded Blaine. "See ya Monday, Terra."

"Okay. Bye."

Walking back, Lisa was silent. Finally, she blurted out: "Why are you smoking, Terra?"

Terra frowned. "I'm not smoking. I mean, it's just the odd one here or there. Like all my friends."

"Not me," Lisa said softly. "Aren't I your friend?"

"Yeah, of course, but you don't live here. I need to fit in with my new friends."

Lisa sighed. "If they were really your friends, wouldn't they accept you how you are? You shouldn't have to change."

"I didn't change!" Terra protested.

"No? Do your parents know you smoke?"

"I told you, I don't smoke. It's not a habit or anything."

"So do your parents know about it?"

Terra shook her head. "Of course not."

"Well, sneaking around and smoking to be cool doesn't sound like the Terra I know. I think you've changed," Lisa said quietly.

Terra felt a bit like yelling and a bit like crying. "Just drop it."

Lisa rubbed the back of her hand on her cheek. "Okay."

The girls were silent as they climbed up the steps into the house and headed up to Terra's bedroom, to wait for Lisa's ride to pick her up.

Dear Diary:

Lisa came to visit today. I thought it was going to be great, but it wasn't.

Lisa doesn't understand how hard it is to make new friends.

And she doesn't understand that things change. I'm getting older. Of course I'm not going to stay exactly the same, right?

She's gone now.

I feel really lonely.

Terra sighed. She closed her diary and went over to the dresser. She pulled out the wrinkled envelope and looked again at the photos of the woman and the baby.

She held the folded note in her hand. She knew what it said, almost by heart. Still, she carefully smoothed the creases and read it again.

Dear baby:

I probably shouldn't even call you a baby, because you'll be much older by the time you're able to read this. But right now, as you lie in the bassinet beside my bed, you are still a very little baby. For tonight only, my baby.

Tomorrow, you'll be handed over to your new parents. I know they are good people, who will love you dearly and who will be able to take good care of you.

Please believe me that this is the right decision for you. I am only seventeen years old, and I'm just not ready to be a mother.

But I want the very best for you, and I will always love you.

Donna Gregory

That was all the note said. Terra paused, looked at the photos again, then put them back in the envelope and shoved it back in the drawer.

She could remember very clearly the day her parents had

given her that envelope.

She'd been about seven years old. Earlier that day, she had come home from school, crying. "Mommy. I told Tina I'm adopted, and she said that means I had another mommy who grew me in her tummy, but didn't want me."

Her mom's eyes filled with tears too. She bent down and hugged Terra very tightly. "Oh, sweetie," she said, "being adopted does mean you grew in another woman's tummy. Remember I told you about Donna?"

Terra nodded. "She was too young to be a mommy."

"Yes. And Mommy and Daddy couldn't make any babies themselves. So Donna chose us to be your parents. We love you very much," said her mother and kissed the young Terra on the forehead.

That evening, her mom and dad came to her bedroom and gave her the photos and letter. They both hugged her and told her again how much they loved her.

"Terra dear," said her mom, "we send a Christmas card every year to Donna, with a recent photo of you. Maybe you'd like to write something in this year's card?"

"No," said Terra, "I don't want to."

"Are you sure?"

Terra nodded vehemently.

Later, Terra had showed the contents of the envelope to Lisa, and they had both cried.

Terra had decided she wasn't going to tell anyone else she was adopted. The girls had clasped hands and sworn to keep it a secret.

At Christmas that same year, her parents had asked her again if she'd like to write in the card to Donna. She'd said no.

Every Christmas since then, they'd repeated the question. Staunchly, she'd always refused.

seven

Sighing, Terra leaned over the smooth wooden banister. She felt the coolness of its curves under her hand. Idly, she watched Fred laying the new hardwood floor in the front entranceway.

"It's a beautiful day," he said, finally. "Why don't you go play outside?"

"I'm fourteen. I'm too old to play."

Fred scratched his head. "Ah, sorry. I didn't know there was an age limit to playing."

"Yeah," answered Terra. "I think it's eleven and under."

He laughed. "I'll make a note of that!" He carefully nailed down a board. "So why are you moping about, anyhow?"

"Hey! I'm not moping!"

"Ah. My mistake. How was your visit with your friend from out of town yesterday?"

She sighed. "It was okay, but not as good as I'd hoped."

"Why not?"

"Well, she doesn't really fit in with my new friends."

"Hmm. Why's that?" Fred's voice was muffled. He was holding several nails between his lips.

Terra shrugged but then realized Fred wasn't looking in her direction. "Um. I don't know."

"Oh...well, Lisa certainly seemed like a nice girl."

"Yeah. Yeah, she is."

"Well, it's important to hang onto good friends when you get them." Fred picked up the hammer and slung it into his belt. He stepped back and surveyed his work. "Looks good, doesn't it?"

Terra didn't answer.

Fred sighed. "If I do say so myself..."

Terra blinked away thoughts of Lisa. "Oh, yeah, it looks good."

Fred nodded and gave her a little wave as he lugged his toolbox into the next room.

*   *   *

Terra stiffened as Joyce and her friends passed her locker. But they didn't even look at her.

Instead they strolled down to the end of the hall and surrounded a small blonde girl. She couldn't hear what they were saying, but she felt sorry for the other kid.

"Somebody should do something about that," said Terra.

"Oh, yeah?" Blaine leaned up against her locker. "Well, you could do like Paula and beat the you-know-what outta her."

"Really?" asked Terra. "I mean, Paula did that?"

"Oh, yeah. Why do you think Joyce stays away from Paula?"

"Because Paula's scary?"

Blaine's laughter rang out, echoing among the lockers. "You bet. That's why!"

Terra looked down the hall. Suddenly, the small girl thrust something at Joyce and ran into the classroom.

"What did she give her?" she asked curiously.

"Probably some money."

"You're kidding, right?"

Blaine shrugged. "No…they bully kids outta stuff; their money, homework, whatever."

"But that's terrible! Can't someone stop them?"

"Why? It's not our problem."

"But it's really awful."

"Yeah, whatever. Come on, eh?"

Terra followed her out of the school. They met up with some of the other kids under the tree in the park. "Hey," said Paula, puffing on a cigarette. She handed it to Terra, who smoked for a few moments, then handed it off to Blaine.

Blaine finished it and crunched it under her heel.

Paula lit another one.

Pete shuffled from one leg to the other. "So?"

"Hmm?" Paula lifted an eyebrow at him.

"Ya coming or what?"

Paula shrugged. "Yeah, sure. Nothing else to do." She stood up to follow Pete, who was already striding off.

She tilted her head at Blaine and Terra. "Well, c'mon."

Terra blinked uncertainly but stood up and walked with the girls across the park. Pete was fiddling with the latch on a small storage shed. It popped open, and he slid inside. Paula followed.

Terra hesitated.

Blaine sighed and tugged her arm. "Come on. It's no big deal."

Pete was sitting cross-legged on the floor, opening a little bag.

Paula handed the cigarette to Terra and sat down beside Pete. "Whadda you got? Any of the good stuff?"

He shook his head. "Just weed. But I'll be getting something else soon, don't you worry."

"Yeah, I bet it will be pricey, though."

"Naw, it's worth it, baby."

Pete grinned and pulled Blaine close to him. He took something out of the bag and rolled it in cigarette paper. He handed it to Paula and she lit it, closing her eyes and taking a deep draw. After a few moments, she offered it to Terra.

Terra could feel her heart racing, and her palms felt sweaty. "Uh, no," she said, lifting up the cigarette she was already holding. "I'm good with this."

Pete stared at her. "So why are you here?"

But Paula just shrugged. "More for us."

The taste of her cigarette, plus the sickly sweet smell of the marijuana, was making Terra feel sick to her stomach. She was so nervous, she thought she might throw up. She kept looking at the door, expecting police or a teacher or her mother to burst through at any moment.

Terra wished she could pass on the cigarette, but she didn't want her hands empty, in case someone offered her the drug again.

Finally, the other kids finished, and the cigarette in Terra's hand was very short.

"You'd better butt that out," said Blaine.

Terra nodded and obediently dropped it on the floor. Blaine stubbed it out with her toe.

"She wasted most of it," Pete grumbled. Blaine elbowed him lightly in the ribs.

Pete took out the bag again and started rolling another joint.

Terra could feel her stomach moving in unpleasant ways. "I'd better get going. I'm expected home soon."

Pete gave a mocking laugh, and Paula waved.

"Bye," said Blaine, leaning close to Pete to watch what he was doing.

Terra slipped through the door and started across the park. Suddenly her stomach turned completely. She fell to her knees and vomited on the ground.

She stood up shakily, wiping her mouth on the back of her hand, just as Glenn came running over.

"Terra. Are you okay?" he sounded really worried.

She felt humiliated. She moved away from the mess on the ground. She wondered if she looked terrible. She knew she must smell.

"Uh, yeah. I guess I just wasn't feeling well. Sorry. How embarrassing."

"Well, don't be embarrassed for being sick." He went to take her arm.

She shook him off, not wanting him close enough to smell her vomit breath. "I'm not sick."

He frowned at her, looking confused. He looked over as the sound of laughter came from the shack. It might have been her imagination, but to Terra, it looked like his face fell slightly. "Terra. What are you doing?"

She flushed. "Nothing. What do you mean?"

"I think you know what I mean."

"I wasn't smoking drugs!"

"Hmm. But you were smoking something?"

"Just a cigarette! No big deal."

"Ah," said Glenn. He looked steadily at her. "And you've got that nervous stomach…"

She nodded.

"I don't have to tell you about how disgusting lung cancer is?"

She shook her head. "I saw the video."

"And you know the whole yellow teeth, yellow fingers thing? Do you really want that?" He raised an eyebrow at her.

51

She gave a little laugh but felt her eyes filling up with tears.

Glenn patted down his pockets and frowned. "I don't have any tissue."

"S'okay," said Terra, through a small sob.

"I've got gum though. You want some gum?"

"Okay," said Terra, taking a deep breath. She took the gum from Glenn. They started to walk across the park to the sidewalk.

"Terra," said Glenn.

She looked at him.

"About the drugs, you might think you won't do it, but it's pretty hard if you're always hanging around kids who are. They make it seem fun, and you don't want to miss out."

"I don't do drugs."

"Yeah? A month ago you told me you didn't smoke either."

"It's none of your business," Terra blurted out.

Glenn stopped and looked at her. He nodded. "You're right. It's not."

He paused. "Well," he waved. "See ya." And he walked off.

Terra stared after him. She felt the tears welling up in her eyes again. She ran home and cried into her pillow.

Dear Diary:

I had a bad day today.

Can you believe I was around drugs? At first it seemed very exciting, like I was in a movie or something. But my stomach felt so nervous, and I threw up.

And Glenn is mad at me. He doesn't like my friends.

I hate Inglewood.

eight

Her father peeled the banana deftly, smoothly slicing it into cereal-sized chunks. He hummed something tuneless under his breath.

Her mother poured liberal portions of orange juice into everyone's glass.

Terra sat at the breakfast table across from her parents. She stared listlessly at her bowl of Cheerios.

"Want some bananas in there?" asked her dad, slicing pieces off into his own bowl.

"I don't care."

"What's wrong?" asked her mom.

"Nothing."

"Do you miss Lisa?"

"No."

"What?" her father blinked. "Isn't she your best friend?"

Terra shrugged. "She doesn't live here."

"Hmm," said her mom. "Well, that friend Blaine you had over seems nice. Didn't she seem nice, dear?"

He nodded, absently cutting into the banana.

"So you're making friends, Terra?" asked her mother persistently.

"Yeah, sure. Yeah."

Her mother pursed her lips. "Still, I think something's wrong. Even Fred noticed it."

Terra sighed. "Fred doesn't even live here."

Her father grinned. "Yeah, but you wouldn't know it! I'm starting to think of him as a fixture in the place. Fred the fixture. Here, Terra, have some bananas." He dumped some slices into her bowl.

But they tasted like nothing. Big soft lumps of nothing.

The phone rang.

"Oh, hi!" said her mom. "We were just talking about you. It was so nice to have you visit last week, dear." She held the phone out to Terra. "It's for you, sweetie."

"Excuse me," said Terra, pushing away from the table. She took the cordless phone and went into her bedroom. "Hello?"

"Hi, Terra. It's Lisa."

Terra swallowed. "Hi."

"How are you?"

"Okay. How are you?"

"Okay too."

"Oh," said Terra.

"That's not true," Lisa burst out. "I'm terrible. I hate that we fought. It's not my place to criticize you or your new friends."

"No, no," said Terra. "You can say whatever you want. You're my best friend."

"It's just that…" Lisa stopped.

"Yes?" said Terra. "Go ahead." She gulped. "I'm sorry. I didn't mean to upset you."

"No, no." It sounded like Lisa was crying too. "I just want you to be happy."

"I am," said Terra. "I will be. Don't worry."

"Okay," Lisa sniffled.

"Listen, I just wanted to say I'm sorry if you didn't have a good time when you were here."

Lisa was quiet for a moment. "I did have a good time, for the most part."

"Oh. Okay. Well. I just wanted to say I'm sorry."

"Okay. Me, too."

Terra frowned. "What are you sorry for?"

Lisa suddenly giggled. "I'm not sure!"

"Oh, well. That's okay then."

There was a short pause, where neither said anything.

"So Terra?"

"Yeah?"

"Are we still best friends?"

Terra smiled into the phone. "Of course, we are."

There was a small pause. "Do you want to hear what Dana did to try and get David's attention?"

"Yeah, sure."

And they chatted like crazy for the next hour, until Lisa's mom finally made her get off the phone.

*   *   *

"Pick up the pace, Blaine!" called Ms. Brown from where she stood beside the track.

Blaine rolled her eyes but kept running.

"Woo, woo," teased Terra, lapping her. "It's weird to see you actually participating in gym class."

"Don't...make me...regret it..." Blaine puffed.

Terra waved and ran across the finish line.

"Good job, Terra," called Ms. Brown. "Don't forget to stretch."

She sat on the bleachers, waiting for Blaine to finish. She was tired, but in a good way. Taking a deep breath, Terra let it out, feeling it drain to the ends of each tingling muscle.

She felt almost a sense of well-being that lasted, well, to biology class.

*   *   *

Terra stared morosely at the dead frog in front of her. "I don't know how much more of this I can take."

"More of what, exactly? Frogs?" Glenn raised an eyebrow at her.

"Crayfish, rats, frogs—all the cutting."

He laughed. "But haven't I been doing most of the cutting?"

"I still have to look at them, and smell them."

"It's mostly the chemicals that you smell."

"Yeah. Still, it's horrible."

"Aw, it's not so bad. At least you're not as white as Chuck." He nodded across the table, where Kaitlin was again holding her frog by the pins, teasing Chuck by making it dance on the table. Chuck had moved his stool several feet away and was staring at the floor.

"It's kind of fun, don't you think?" asked Kaitlin.

"No," answered Terra honestly.

Kaitlin smiled. "It's kinda neat trying to figure out how all the systems in their bodies work. It's quite incredible, actually."

"I guess… I don't have the stomach for that kind of work, I don't think."

"Chuck definitely doesn't," grinned Glenn. "Eh, Chuck?"

Chuck didn't look up from the floor.

"Don't tease him!" Kaitlin admonished. "I'm wearing new shoes."

Terra couldn't help herself; she burst out laughing.

"So did Glenn ask you about Friday night?" Kaitlin smiled.

Terra hesitated, glanced at Glenn. "No…"

He blushed and shot Kaitlin a dark look. "I was getting to it."

Kaitlin chuckled.

"So Terra," said Glenn, cutting open the frog. "Some of the kids are coming over to my place Friday evening. I was wondering if you wanted to come along?"

Terra, who was staring at the frog as Glenn started to pin back its skin to expose the organs inside, blinked.

"It's no big deal," said Glenn quickly. "You don't have to."

"No, no. I'd like to come."

She looked across the table to see Kaitlin grinning at her.

*   *   *

"Well, are his parents going to be home?" queried her mom.

"He didn't mention it. I guess so, though."

"Hmm," said her mom, exchanging glances with her dad across the kitchen table.

"Is this a boyfriend, Terra?" asked her dad.

"No, no! He's just a nice guy. Besides, other kids are going to be there."

"Hmm," said her mom. "Okay, tell you what. I'll drop you off and I'll take just a moment to meet his parents."

"Mom!" Terra rolled her eyes. "How embarrassing!"

"It sounds reasonable, Terra," her dad said.

"Makes sense to me!" piped in Fred from the corner of the kitchen, packing up his tools for the day. "It's good to see parents looking out for their kids."

Terra groaned and dropped her forehead onto the table.

*   *   *

"It's really okay, Mom," Terra protested as her mother followed her up to Glenn's front door.

"No, no." Her mom was resolute. "I want to meet his parents. I won't stay, I promise."

Terra sighed, and rang the bell. A grey-haired gentleman opened the door. He looked over the top of his glasses at her, smiling. "I'm guessing you must be Terra." He gestured them inside.

He turned his attention to her mother. "Ah, you brought a friend! And who is this young lady?"

Terra rolled her eyes as her mother actually blushed. "Oh, my. I'm Terra's mother, Sharon."

"Nice to meet you! I'm Glenn's Grandpa. Grandpa Bob, the kids call me. Won't you come in?"

"Oh, no—I just thought I'd take a moment to meet Glenn's parents before I left Terra for her visit. But if you're here—I just wanted to make sure there'd be adult supervision."

"Of course!" Grandpa Bob smiled. "Glenn actually lives with his Grandma and me."

As if on cue, a woman appeared at his side, wiping her hands on her apron. Her long grey hair was tied back in a neat bun, although a small curl escaped at her temple. "Hi! I'm Lorna." She shook hands with her guests and beamed at Terra. "I've been wanting to meet you; Glenn's been talking about you these past few weeks!"

"Grandma!" Glenn's face was red as he bounded up the stairs into the lobby, with Winter behind him.

"Hi, Terra," he said, a bit sheepishly. Then he stepped forward and firmly shook Terra's mom's hand. "It's nice to meet you."

"You too." She smiled at him. "Of course, I've seen you before when you've walked Terra home. I was peeking out my office window."

"Mom!" It was Terra's turn to be embarrassed.

The adults all laughed.

"Hey," said Winter. She smiled at Terra's mom. "Hi, Mrs. Morrison. My mother said to tell you we could drop Terra off later, if that's all right with you."

Her mother hesitated. "What time do you think you'll be going home?"

"Oh, no later than ten. Is that okay?"

"Well, it's not a school night, so yes. Thanks, Winter." Terra's mom turned to go down the steps. "It was very nice to meet you all."

"Don't you want to stay for a while?" asked Grandpa Bob.

She looked at Terra and shook her head, smiling. "No, but thank you. Have a good time, Terra."

Terra followed Glenn and Winter down into the basement, where Kaitlin, Tracy, Chuck and another boy named Brad were already listening to CDs and munching on chocolate chip cookies.

"Hi, Terra!" smiled Kaitlin, from under the brim of a large purple hat.

"That's a nice hat."

Tilting one edge of the hat in Terra's direction, Kaitlin nodded. "Hats are one of my props."

"What do you mean?"

"Well, it's something to be known for. Like, if someone doesn't know me, and you say: 'The girl who's always wearing cool hats...' they might go 'Oh yeah, I've seen her. ...'"

"Maybe they say: 'Oh yeah, the girl with the stupid hats,'" grinned Tracy.

"Oooh, that hurts," said Kaitlin. "Winter?"

"Naw, you look great, girl."

Kaitlin grinned. "Yeah, of course I do. Anyway, Tracy's

just bitter because she doesn't have a good prop."

"You took my puppy away!"

"You weren't looking after him properly," countered Kaitlin.

"Kaitlin lent Tracy a little stuffed dog to carry around as a prop for a while," explained Winter.

"Oh."

"But not everyone needs props."

Kaitlin hooted. "What do you call those?" She gestured to Winter's striped stockings.

Winter just grinned.

"Hmm, I don't have any props," Terra said uncertainly.

Winter waved her hand dismissively. "Never mind that idiosyncrasy."

Kaitlin rolled her eyes. "So I have a foible."

"Enough already," moaned Brad.

"No, really," interjected Kaitlin. "You ought to have a prop, Terra. How about a scarf?"

Winter laughed. "At least it would keep you warm."

"No," protested Kaitlin. "A perfectly useless silk scarf…maybe in earth tones, to go with her name. Maybe you should try to capitalize on that whole earthy thing, Terra."

"Well…" Terra wasn't sure if they were making fun of her, but Kaitlin seemed in earnest, even though she was smiling.

"I really like your name," said Glenn softly, standing just behind her.

Terra could feel a blush creeping across her cheeks. Her heart rate picked up a notch.

Winter flopped down on the sofa. "I like to call this a chesterfield."

"What?"

"You know, the couch, the sofa. It's a Canadian word, not American. But it's dying out. So we need to use it more."

"Chesterfield…" repeated Terra. "My parents say that sometimes."

But just then, Glenn's grandparents came downstairs, each carrying an armful of treats.

"Woo woo!" shouted Winter, jumping up to help them deposit the goodies on the side table.

At Glenn's encouragement, Terra helped herself to a glass of orange pop and some potato chips.

Glenn's grandparents sat down on the…chesterfield. To Terra's surprise, no one seemed to mind having the adults there.

"Grandpa Bob!" exclaimed Winter. "Won't you tell us one of your stories?"

He smiled at her. "Ah Winter… I'm not sure if I have any, off the top of my head. Let me think about it…"

He tilted his head to one side for a moment, then began: "Okay, here's a true story. Once there was a young man who thought he had everything together. He had a beautiful young wife and a good job. Everything was going great.

"But then, he met up with some new friends who liked to party and drink a lot. So instead of coming home after work, he used to meet up with his friends and drink. Mostly they just drank, but sometimes some of them got rowdy and got into fights or other trouble. Most of them drove drunk.

"One day, one of the young man's best friends drove right into a tree and died. That was so depressing for the young man, but he just drank even more. He had a hard time getting up in the mornings and couldn't concentrate properly. He lost his job.

"One morning he woke up and realized his wife too had

gone. Finally, he realized he had to make some changes in his life. He asked God for forgiveness. Then he got counselling and help to quit drinking. And then he had to ask his wife for forgiveness too…"

"Did she forgive him?" Tracy interjected.

"Oh, yes." Grandpa Bob squeezed his wife's hand. She gazed fondly at him.

"Did they have kids?" Tracy asked.

"Oh, yes, even grandkids," Grandma Lorna answered, with a warm smile for Glenn.

"So everything worked out, then."

"Well, yes, Tracy, thank God . But a lot of heartache could have been spared if that young man had just made the right choices in the first place. And he could have been a better influence on his friends, like the man who was killed, to help them make better choices too."

Grandpa Bob smiled at the kids. "You guys are still young, and you have the opportunity to make good choices right off the bat."

"That's cool, Grandpa Bob," Winter nodded at him.

Grandpa Bob smiled at her. "I think that's enough of the old people, hmm?" He got up, brushed the creases out of his pants, and offered his arm to his wife. "Grandma Lorna? We should leave the kids to watch their movie."

Together, they serenely climbed the stairs.

"Aren't they just great?" asked Kaitlin. "You're so lucky, Glenn."

Glenn smiled. "Yeah, I guess I am. Thanks."

Winter frowned as she loaded up the DVD player. "This is some sort of action-comedy thing. I hope it's okay."

"As long as it's not gory, eh Chuck?" Kaitlin teased.

Chuck blushed and tossed a pillow at her, which of course

started an impromptu pillow fight. Finally, Kaitlin, Tracy and Chuck squeezed into the loveseat to watch the movie.

Someone turned down the lights. Winter sat down beside Brad on the overstuffed chesterfield and patted the seat beside her for Terra. That left just one more space, beside Terra, and Glenn sat in it.

The movie wasn't gory, but Terra had a hard time concentrating. She was very aware of Glenn, sitting close beside her. Then she felt him take her hand in his. "Okay?" he whispered softly.

She looked at him. His eyes, reflected in the glow of the television, looked very blue. Terra nodded, and he smiled at her. She felt his hand relax slowly in hers.

But it was very hard to concentrate on the movie.

* * *

Later, after the movie, she sat alone with Glenn on the chesterfield. "Where are your parents?" she asked, softly.

"Ah." Glenn leaned back against the armrest. "Well, we used to live in Edmonton, but when I was eleven, my Dad took off."

Terra wasn't sure what to say. "I'm sorry."

"It's okay." He shook his head. "Well, it wasn't okay—it sucked, actually. But I'm used to it now. Anyhow, my mom was kind of a mess afterwards, and I was too, really. So we moved here with Grandma and Grandpa. But then, my mom got offered a promotion at her old job in Edmonton, and she decided to take it. I was in the middle of the school year then, and we decided I'd stay here. And we've just gone on like that."

"But isn't that weird? Living apart from your mom too?"

He shrugged. "She visits most weekends. I think she's still trying to get it together, really. But my grandparents are great. They've helped me get my head on straight. More or less."

"Do you see your dad?"

He shook his head. "He used to visit every now and then. But it's been about a year since I've seen him."

"Wow. I'm sorry."

He smiled. "I'm doing okay." Glenn paused. "Hey, listen. I'm really sorry I came down on you so hard about the smoking and drugs thing. You've got to make your own decisions."

Terra looked at him seriously. "I don't think I've been making the best decisions."

"Hmm. Well, it's not too late to start."

"Yeah?"

"Of course. I mean, I know firsthand. I've messed up. It took me a while to figure out for myself that drugs were bad news." He squinted. "Well, actually Grandpa grounded me until I figured it out. Still, like he told me—it's eventually up to us to be the kind of people we really want to be." He shrugged. "And that's not who I wanted to be."

"So are you the kind of person you want to be now?"

He laughed. "No, unfortunately! But I'm working on it."

She smiled at him.

"Seriously, though. There's also the Kaitlin angle to think about."

Terra frowned, confused. "What does it have to do with Kaitlin? She doesn't smoke, does she?"

"No, definitely not. Neither did her mother. But her grandparents did."

"I don't understand."

He shook his head. "Well, you wouldn't, I guess, unless

somebody told you. Kaitlin's mom died of cancer when Kaitlin was just a little kid, and they figure second-hand smoke had something to do with it. So the gang's pretty adamantly against smoking."

Terra nodded. "That's really sad."

"Yeah," said Glenn. "It's been hard on Kaitlin." He glanced at her. "Besides, smoking made you sick, didn't it?"

Terra shrugged, sighed. "Sort of. But it's more the nervous stomach."

"So tell me again; what's with that?"

"Well, that's what my mom calls it. If I feel uncomfortable with a situation, I…"

"You puke?"

"Ah, yeah, I guess I do."

He grinned. "That is so cool. Hey, between you and Chuck—if he has to cut something up in biology, or if you have a guilty conscience or are nervous—either way, I'd better watch my shoes."

She blushed, looked away.

"Hey, Terra. I'm just teasing."

"Yeah. I know."

They sat silently. Terra's brain tried to process the events and discussion of the evening.

Glenn took her hand between both of his. Terra felt suddenly shy as Glenn looked deeply into her eyes.

He moved a little closer.

Terra swallowed.

"Hey, TERRA!" shouted Winter, grinning as she came down the stairs. Terra and Glenn dropped hands guiltily.

"It's almost ten. My mom is here to take us home."

"Ah. Right." Glenn walked the girls to the door. "See ya at school."

"Yeah," Terra repeated. "See you at school…"

"Oh, Terra, Terra…" Winter's eyes were teasing as she pulled Terra to the vehicle.

Dear Diary:

Can you believe it? Glenn held my hand tonight. I think he must like me. Wow.

It only made me feel a little bit sick to my stomach, but in a good way.

Kaitlin and Winter seem really nice; I'm not so sure about Tracy.

Still, it was a very nice night. Did I tell you?—GLENN HELD MY HAND!!

nine

Sighing, Terra sat on the stairwell landing, halfway between upstairs and downstairs, and watched Fred nail freshly stained baseboards to the bottom of the wall.

Dressed in his big blue overalls, he was leisurely tapping in the nails, every so often stepping back to view his work. "Hmm…it looks pretty good, doesn't it?"

"If you do say so yourself?" she asked wryly.

He laughed. "Well, if I don't say it, maybe no one else will! Why not?"

"It does look nice," admitted Terra. "But these house renovations are taking a long time!"

He shrugged, smiling amicably. "If you want it done right…"

"You have to do it yourself?"

Fred looked momentarily alarmed. He shook his head and grinned. "No! You have to hire Fred to do it, and he takes his time—to make sure it's done right."

"Ah." Terra shrugged. She moved down one stair, sunk her chin in her palms, and her elbows on her knees.

She sighed.

Startled, Fred squinted at her. "Anything wrong?"

"No…" She paused. "Not really."

"Hmm…" said Fred, leaning down to pound in another

nail. "So didn't your friend Blaine call, to see if you want to go out?"

"Yeah."

"You don't want to?"

"Not really. I mean, I don't know."

Fred carefully laid his hammer on the stairs and turned his full attention to her. "What's the problem, Terra? You don't like Blaine?"

Terra frowned. "No, I do like her, actually. But I'm not so sure about some of her other friends, and…"

"And what?"

"Well," she whispered. "Some of the stuff they do, I guess."

"Ah," said Fred.

Terra thought he was going to ask for more details, but he didn't. He slowly picked up the hammer and banged in another nail.

"It's important to find the right friends, Terra. You know—people who will support your goals and values, to help you be the kind of person you want to be."

"Yeah. That's funny, someone else just said something along those lines to me…"

Fred sighed. "And here I thought I was original." But he smiled. "So, does that sound like Blaine and her friends?"

She sighed. "Not really."

"Hmm," said Fred. "But they're your best friends at your new school?"

She nodded.

"Ah. That's really tough."

She looked at him to see if he was making fun of her, but he seemed totally serious. "What do you think I should do?"

He shook his shaggy head. "I can't tell you what to do,

Terra. You're a smart girl. I think you know what feels right and what doesn't. Just remember to listen to that little voice."

Terra sighed and made a face. "It's not a voice."

He raised an eyebrow. "Oh? What is it?"

"It's a feeling in my stomach, that makes me want to throw up." She tilted her head. "Of course, sometimes I also want to throw up when something is scary, but it's still a good thing. But when it's bad, I definitely want to throw up."

He held his belly, laughing so hard that Terra's mom opened her office door and peered down at them.

They smiled at her, and she smiled too, then disappeared back into her office.

"So," Fred lowered his voice. "Do you actually throw up?"

"Yeah," Terra grinned broadly. "Sometimes I do."

"Wow," said Fred. "Well, you definitely need to pay attention to that feeling. Otherwise, things are bound to get messy."

"Yeah," agreed Terra. "Very gross."

"Oh! I almost forgot." Fred dug deep into his pocket and brought out some sort of shiny marker. "I got this for you. If you want to outline some of your stars and planets with this, then they'll glow in the dark."

Terra jumped up and took the marker from him. "Wow." She stared at it for a moment. "That is so cool! Thanks, Fred." She ran up the stairs, two at a time, to her room.

"You're welcome." Fred took out another nail and hammered it into the baseboard.

*   *   *

"Hi there!" called Kaitlin as Terra walked down the hallway on the way to her locker.

"Oh. Hi!"

Kaitlin sat on the floor cross-legged, leaning against the lockers, writing on a small notepad. She wore a floppy velvet hat.

Terra paused and looked down at her.

"Are you doing homework?"

"Naw." She closed the book and smiled. "I'm just writing a little note to a friend of mine in France."

"France! Wow. A penpal?"

Kaitlin gave a little laugh. "Well, I guess you could say that. So, did you have a good time at Glenn's the other night?"

"Yeah. It was fun. You've been there before?"

"Sure. Many times." Kaitlin smiled at Terra.

Terra nodded and indicated her armful of books. "Well, I'd better get these to my locker. They weigh a ton."

"I hear ya! See you later."

Terra waved.

*   *   *

"Hey, Terra." Blaine was waiting, leaning against her locker. "So are you coming or what?"

"Coming where?"

Blaine frowned. "To the park. Where else?"

"Oh. No, I don't think so."

"Why not?"

Terra paused. She had an uneasy feeling in her stomach. She didn't want to go, but she didn't want to hurt Blaine's feelings either. "I need to get home."

"You sure?"

"Yeah."

"Oh." Blaine shrugged, grabbed her bag. "Well, okay. See ya then."

"Hi!"

Terra turned around to see Tracy standing there. She was actually surprised to see Tracy coming to talk. She'd had the impression that Tracy wasn't crazy about her.

"Um…hi. How are you?"

Tracy tossed her hair. "Oh, fine."

"Oh. Well." Terra paused, uncertain. "It's nice to see you."

"Yeah, whatever." Tracy stood in front of her locker. "Hey, listen. I just wanted to talk to you about Glenn."

"Glenn?" Terra echoed.

"Yeah, I don't think it's very good of you to take him from Kaitlin. I thought you liked her."

"What? I do like Kaitlin."

"Yeah?" said Tracy, skeptically. "Well, friends don't take friends' guys."

Terra frowned. "Are you saying they're going out? Glenn and Kaitlin?"

It didn't seem to make sense. Glenn hadn't acted…attached, and Kaitlin had been really friendly. Hadn't she?

Tracy just looked at her.

"No one ever told me that," Terra protested.

"Well. Now you know."

"Oh," said Terra, feeling ill again. What was going on?

*　　*　　*

The next day, Blaine stopped by Terra's locker. "Woo." She pushed her long hair away from her face. "That math class was sooo boring, wasn't it?"

"Yeah," Terra acknowledged. "It was pretty dull."

"I hate algebra." Blaine idly fiddled with the lock on the locker beside Terra's.

To their surprise, it came open in her hand. "Woo!" Blaine quickly opened the door and peered inside. "I wonder if there's anything good in here?"

"Blaine! Shut it!"

She laughed. "Why? They left it open!"

"Please, just close it."

Blaine stared at her, closed the door and snapped the lock shut. "Man. You're no fun. Paula woulda had a field day in there."

"Thanks," said Terra, quietly. She stared at her running shoe. There was a small hole in the toe, and her sock showed through.

"So are you coming?"

"To the park?"

"Yeah, of course."

She shook her head. She could feel an uncomfortable prickling behind her eyeballs. "No, I don't think so."

"You're too good for us, or what?"

Terra shook her head again.

"You don't like the gang?"

"No, it's not that. I just don't want to get into the smoking and stuff."

"And stuff?" Blaine's voice sounded mocking.

Terra shrugged.

"You smoked too."

"Yeah. I know. But I don't think I want to any more."

Blaine shoved her hands into her pockets. "Well, we didn't make you do it, you know."

"I know."

"You can still come hang out."

"Yeah. But I think I'd better get home and do some homework. Algebra, you know," she tried lamely joking.

Blaine tossed her hair over her shoulder. "You do what you have to do, Miss Goody-two-shoes."

"Blaine!" Terra protested. "It's nothing personal!"

She gave Terra a dark look. "Yeah, right." She strode down the hall without looking back.

"Hey," said Glenn. "Everything okay?" He glanced down the hall after Blaine.

"Yeah." Terra wasn't sure what to say to him. They hadn't really seen much of each other since that night at his house. And then, after the talk with Tracy...

"So, can I walk you home?"

Terra thought of Kaitlin. She sighed. Kaitlin was a really nice girl.

"No...I don't think that's a very good idea."

He looked confused. "It isn't?"

Terra felt tears filling up her eyelids. She was afraid to blink. "No. Listen...I gotta go."

And, just like that, she walked away.

*   *   *

But Glenn wasn't easily deterred. Wherever Terra went over the next couple of days, she seemed to run into him—in the cafeteria, at the library, in the hallways.

Just as she was thinking about that, he suddenly materialized in front of her. "Hey there." He leaned against the locker beside hers.

"Hi." She glanced at him, feeling a bit uncertain.

"I haven't seen much of you for a few days."

"Yeah."

"Hmm." He gave her a quizzical look. "I was wondering if you wanted to hang out. Maybe go for a walk or something after school."

She stared at him. "It sounds nice, Glenn. But…what about Kaitlin?"

"What about her?"

She just shook her head and picked up her books.

"You want me to ask Kaitlin to come along too?" he called after her.

She frowned at him, exasperated, and walked away.

"Hey!" he called. "Hey, Terra!"

She took a deep breath and hurried off to class without looking back.

*   *   *

At lunch the next day, Terra sat down at the nearest empty table. She smiled as Blaine approached, carrying her tray.

"Hey, Blaine!" she called out.

The girl paused, nodded briefly and headed to the other end of the cafeteria.

Terra felt stricken. She hadn't wanted to lose her new friend. She just didn't want to get into the stuff those kids were doing.

Just then, Kaitlin and Winter appeared, carrying their trays. "Hi, Terra!" said Kaitlin.

"Hi!

"Hey," said Winter.

"Over here, guys!" yelled Tracy from several tables away.

"Oh," Kaitlin paused. "Well, we'll talk to you later."

"Yeah," said Terra, as the girls gave her warm smiles and left. Glenn and Chuck came into the cafeteria. Tracy called them over too. Glenn glanced questioningly at Terra before following Chuck to join the girls.

She stared down at her unappetizing food—a barely warm pile of macaroni and cheese, and wondered if she was going to be sick.

Dear Diary:

I think I've lost my new friends, including Blaine. I wonder if I made a mistake. After all, Blaine's right; they never forced me to do anything.

I hate living here. This is too hard.

I miss Lisa.

* * *

Terra hesitated as she walked into the library. Kaitlin sat there, in a broad straw hat, scribbling furiously on a piece of paper.

She thought of just quietly slipping by, but Kaitlin looked up and patted the spot beside her. "Hey, Terra. Have a seat."

"Hi." She slipped into the chair beside Kaitlin.

Kaitlin tilted the hat back and looked directly at Terra. "So," she said, "what's going on with Glenn?"

Terra blinked. She was surprised Kaitlin had brought it up so directly.

"Nothing. Really nothing."

"Oh," said Kaitlin, frowning slightly.

"And—I just want you to know—I had no idea about you guys."

Kaitlin frowned. "What do you mean?"

"You and Glenn."

The crease between Kaitlin's eyebrows deepened. "What?"

"I didn't know that you guys were—going out, or whatever."

"Me neither! That is, we're not! Why would you think that?"

Terra felt flustered. "Uh, someone told me that."

Kaitlin hesitated a moment then turned the paper in front of her towards Terra.

Dear Michael,
    How are you? Or, should I say: "Comment ça va?"
    How has your week been? Mine's been okay, but I still miss you so much...

"I haven't got very far with this one yet. I write him at least once a week."

"Oh," said Terra, trying to grasp the significance of this. "This is your boyfriend?"

Kaitlin shrugged, smiled a bit. "I wish he was. He moved away. He and his mom are living in France now, so who knows when we'll see each other again. We're just friends. Special friends. I feel like I can write him anything. He used to live next door to me, but they moved away after his dad died." She paused, then brightened. "But they still own that house. They're just renting it out right now."

"So he might come back?"

"Yeah…" For once, Kaitlin looked totally serious. "At least, I really hope so."

"You really like him, eh?"

She smiled. "Yeah, I guess so. But we're doing totally different things now. I mean, France! Wow. You know?"

Terra smiled. "Yeah."

"He goes to a private school and does all kinds of sports.

Especially soccer, but they call it football over there."

"Yeah, I heard that. It's kind of confusing."

"Yeah." Kaitlin sighed. "Actually, his mom has a French boyfriend now."

"Really? Does Michael like him?"

"Michael writes that he's nice enough. It's hard to tell with letters sometimes. I know about that though, right? I had a tough time for a long time with my stepmother."

"You like her now?"

Kaitlin smiled ruefully. "Most days. No, really, Jane's pretty great."

"You're the only kid?"

"No. I have a sister, half-sister really. "

"How old?"

"Hmm. Six now."

"That must be fun. I wish I had a sister," said Terra wistfully.

Kaitlin scrunched up her face. "She's pretty annoying, actually." Then she relented. "But yeah, she can be kinda sweet too."

They sat quietly for a moment. "Um…does Glenn know about Michael?"

"Of course. They know each other. We all went to school together."

Terra, frowning, tried to remember exactly what Tracy had told her. "Are you sure Glenn doesn't like you?"

"Not like that. I'm pretty sure." Kaitlin stood up suddenly, tucked the notepad under one arm and grabbed Terra's hand. "Come, come with me."

"What?" protested Terra, half-dragged along behind Kaitlin.

"Just come this way."

She stopped in the hallway, where several kids were hanging around in front of their lockers. Glenn was talking to Brad and Chuck. Tracy was pasting little stickers on her locker door.

"Hey, Glenn," called out Kaitlin.

Terra moaned to herself. "Kaitlin, never mind," she whispered.

Kaitlin just smiled at her.

"Uh. Yes, Kaitlin?" Glenn leaned against the locker, watching them.

"Do you like me?"

He grinned. "Yeah, sure, Kaitlin. I like ya."

She sighed, exasperated, and stamped her foot on the ground. Her hat fell over her eyes and she pushed it back. "That's not what I mean. I mean, do you LIKE-like me?"

"Oh." He straightened up, frowned slightly, his gaze travelling to Terra, then back to Kaitlin. "No offence, kid, but no..."

She nodded pleased. She patted Glenn on the arm. "No problemo! Just checking."

She pulled Terra a little further down the hall. "See? Have we got that settled?"

Terra felt incredibly embarrassed. She wondered if she looked as red as she felt. She glanced back at Tracy, who was staring blankly at her. And Glenn too, was standing in the hall, staring at the retreating girls.

"Yeah. Um. Yeah."

Terra could still feel her skin burning as Kaitlin laughed, as if it were enormously funny.

Later, Glenn caught up with her, as she was just leaving the school. "Terra!"

She turned around shyly. "Hi."

"I'd ask you if I could walk you home, but I'm afraid of

what you might say this time."

She blushed. "Yeah. I'm sorry."

"I'm getting the impression that maybe you thought I was going out with Kaitlin or something like that?"

"Uh, yeah."

"I just don't understand why you thought that."

"Well," Terra hesitated, "I guess because Tracy told me you were."

"Tracy did? Huh." He paused. "That doesn't surprise me, she's a bit protective."

Terra blinked. "Of you?"

"No!" Glenn laughed. "Of Kaitlin. They've been best friends for a long time, but sometimes I think Tracy is a bit too protective of that relationship. Or something like that." He shrugged. "But I wouldn't worry about it."

She nodded and smiled shyly at him. "So, you don't like-like Kaitlin?"

He shook his head. "Naw. Although..." he paused, glancing over at her. "Just to be perfectly honest, I was kind of keen on her a couple of years ago. But nothing came of it—she was totally into this other guy, Michael."

"Yeah, she told me a bit about him. They write letters."

"Ah, okay. I wasn't sure if they were still in touch. He's a good guy though. But we were all just kids back then," he added.

Terra laughed. "Aren't we still kids at fourteen?"

He smiled. "I guess it depends on how you look at it. To my grandparents, we're kids. Then again, they may still think of me as a kid when I'm thirty! I'm actually fifteen, though. He glances sideways at her. "I'll be getting my driver's licence next year."

"That's so cool."

"Yeah, it is, isn't it?" He grinned broadly. "My Grandpa already told me he'll let me drive his car; I just have to take a driver's ed course, once I have my birthday."

He smiled at her, and Terra could feel herself blushing. "But you, Terra, you're still a kid," he teased.

"Yeah, I think so. I mean, when I stop being a kid, I have to give up going out for Halloween!"

"What? You still go out?"

"Well, the year before last, I didn't go. But then last year, my friend Lisa and I thought we'd take our last chance to go out before we were definitely too old."

"Hey, that's cool. I think anyone who wants to should be able to trick-or-treat. As long as they dress up, though. Hey, you dressed up, didn't you?"

"Of course! We went as mimes, painted our faces white and all that."

"Ah. I bet you looked great." He smiled at her.

Terra smiled back.

Dear Diary:
  Wanna know a secret?
  I kind of like Glenn.
  And I think he likes me too. Isn't that exciting?

ten

Terra took a deep breath, and before she could lose her nerve, walked over to Tracy's locker—the neatest one Terra had ever seen—with special additional shelving inside, and color coding—so each binder fit into a designated spot. The inside of the door was covered with tiny stickers; mainly flowers and unicorns.

She tried for her friendliest smile. "Hi, Tracy."

Tracy tossed her dark bangs away from her eyes and gave Terra a wary look. "Uh, hi."

"So. How are you doing?"

"Okay, I guess." She paused. "And ah, you?"

"I'm okay too, thanks. I was wondering if you had a partner yet for that history project?"

Before Tracy could open her mouth, Terra added: "I mean, Kaitlin and Winter aren't in our class, so I was wondering if you'd paired up with anybody yet?"

"I, uh…" Tracy looked uncomfortable. Terra was sure she was going to refuse the offer. But the other girl shifted slightly, a confused expression on her face. "You really want to be my partner?"

"Yeah, sure," Terra nodded.

"Oh.

There was a long silence. "Well?" Terra prompted quietly. "What do you think?"

"You sure?"

"Yeah."

"Well, okay." For the first time ever, Tracy smiled at Terra. "Thanks."

Terra nodded. "Okay. Well, I guess we can talk about it more after we get more details in class." She gave a little wave and started to move away, but Tracy called after her.

"Terra?"

"Yes?"

Tracy took a step closer, and lowered her voice. "I guess I probably shouldn't have said that, about Kaitlin and Glenn."

"Oh. Well...that's okay."

"I didn't make it up," Tracy added quickly. "He did like her—but it was a long time ago."

"Ah…okay. It doesn't matter."

"Anyway, Kaitlin likes another guy."

"Ah," said Terra.

Tracy smiled. "And I guess Glenn likes another girl, eh?"

Terra looked at the cracks in the floor. "Oh?"

"He's really nice," Tracy whispered, before running back to her locker. "See you in history class!"

*   *   *

Glenn was waiting by her locker after school. "Hey there."

"Hi." She fumbled to undo her lock. She tried to remember which books she needed for her homework, but she was so distracted, that she just dumped a bunch of them into her backpack.

"You're pretty keen, hmm?"

"What?"

"You're taking home the biology textbook to study? I don't think we had any biology homework."

"Oh. Right." She blushed. "I, um, forgot." She took the heavy book out of her backpack and threw it into the bottom of her locker.

"Good," he grinned. "Because I was going to offer to carry that, and that book weighs a ton."

She giggled. "Yeah. We should sue. Damage to our bodies or something. But I can carry it myself."

"Sure. Don't say I didn't offer!"

"Okay. I'm not going to offer to carry yours, though!"

"No? What if I was on crutches?"

"Yeah, if you were on crutches, I'd probably offer."

"What if I was just really really tired?"

"Nope."

"No? That's kind of cruel!"

"Ah, well!" She grinned at him, as they walked out of the school.

"You want to go sit in the park across the street for a bit?"

She nodded. "Sure. I'm not in a big rush. Well, I'm supposed to call home if I'm going to—as my mom says—'dawdle' past four o'clock. But I have a bit of time."

"Cool."

They walked slowly across the park. Terra couldn't help looking over at the little shack in the distance.

Glenn noticed. "You haven't been hanging out with that bunch much lately?"

She shook her head. "No. I kind of miss Blaine, though. But she's mad at me, because I don't really want to do some of the stuff they do."

He nodded. "Yeah, those kind of things are tough. I pretty

much lost some of my friends, because I wasn't wanting to drink or whatever any more."

"But couldn't you still be friends, though?"

"Yeah, and I'm still sort of friends with a couple of them. But not like before. It's hard, if you don't share the same interests."

Terra nodded. "Yeah, I guess so. So what are your interests?"

"We-l-l..." Glenn said. "I'm looking at a big one right now."

She blushed and he laughed.

"Really though, I like to play basketball. I like cars. My Grandpa lets me help tinker around with his, so that's kind of fun. I'd love to rebuild some sort of old car some day. What else? I like hockey, I guess."

"To play?"

He shook his head. "Naw, not so much, although I play a mean game of street hockey. But I never really got into the ice hockey thing."

"And you call yourself a Canadian?" she teased.

He laughed. "Hey, I'm plenty patriotic. I've wrapped myself in a giant Canadian flag and run naked through the streets on Canada Day."

"You have not!" She paused uncertainly and looked curiously at him. "Did you?"

"Um. Well...actually my Grandma forced me to wear shorts. But I'm sure I looked like I was naked, except for the flag."

She giggled. "That must have been something to see."

He nodded and grinned. "I did it a few years in a row. I'm telling you, the neighbours expect it now. You can see them on Canada Day, peering over their front fences to see if I'm coming."

Terra shook her head, laughing. "You'd better not tell my parents that, if you're visiting at my place!"

"Oh? So does that mean I'm invited?"

She glanced at him. "Do you want to?"

"Of course!"

"Oh. Well, okay then." She smiled at him.

Just then, they heard a shout. Paula came running over. She stopped, gasping for breath. Her face was really white. "I don't know what to do. Blaine's in trouble. She won't wake up. I thought she was just tired, but I don't know how to wake her up." Then she burst out in sobs.

"Whoa," said Glenn, getting up from the bench. He put a hand on Paula's shoulder. "Start again. Where is she?"

Paula pointed frantically at the shack. "In there."

Glenn nodded. "Okay, let's go."

Paula took off at a run for the shack, and Glenn and Terra raced after her.

Blaine lay crumpled in a small heap on the dirt floor of the little shack. Pete leaned languidly against the far wall.

"Blaine!" Terra shouted, but there was no response.

"S'okay," said Pete. "She's just sleeping it off. No big deal. S'okay."

Glenn bent over her. "She's breathing, thank God. Blaine, Blaine, can you hear me?"

There was no response. Terra could feel her own heart beating wildly, as tears pricked at her eyelids.

Meanwhile Paula dashed around in small circles, moaning. "Is she dying? Is she dying?"

"Ah, pipe down," said Pete, dragging on his cigarette.

"What did you give her?" Glenn asked Pete.

He shrugged. "I don't know. Nothing much."

"Pills," said Paula. "It was some pills."

Glenn shoved Pete's shoulder.

"Hey!" Pete protested.

"What did you give her?" yelled Glenn.

"I don't remember!" shouted Pete. "Leave me alone!"

Terra dropped to her knees beside Blaine. "Glenn! Help her!"

Glenn ran back to her and lifted Blaine's head under her neck, tilting it back. "I heard this in health class—first aid," he muttered.

He dug into his coat jacket, pulled out a cell phone and dialled 911. "Hello! There's an unconscious girl here. I think it's a drug overdose... Yeah. In the park across the street from Inglewood Junior High School. There's a small shack there. We're inside."

He put down the phone. "Okay, they're on their way."

Pete blinked, stood up uncertainly. "Who'd ya call? The cops?"

"An ambulance," Glenn said shortly.

"Bet there will be cops," said Pete. "I'm outta here!"

"Hey!" said Glenn. "The ambulance guys will want to talk to you."

"No way, bro." Pete stumbled out of the door. "I'm out of here."

"Blaine! Blaine!" Paula screeched, still pacing.

Terra held tightly to Blaine's hand. It felt limp and cold in hers. "Come on, Blaine," she whispered. "It's going to be okay." She could feel the tears running down her cheeks.

Glenn's face was white too.

They heard the sound of sirens in the distance.

"I can't get in trouble with the cops," whispered Paula.

Terra just stared at her.

"I...I gotta go." And Paula disappeared too.

Glenn sighed heavily. He gently brushed the hair out of Blaine's face, then touched Terra's arm. "I'm going to go wave them in here. I'll be right back."

She nodded wordlessly and stayed crouched beside Blaine.

*　　*　　*

Everything after that was a blur—a big rush of paramedics and stretchers, sirens and flashing lights.

"Are you two coming?" somebody asked, and Glenn must have answered, because Terra suddenly felt herself being boosted into the back of the ambulance. It smelled funny in there, like cleaners maybe, and something else Terra couldn't recognize.

They put some sort of mask over Blaine's face—for oxygen, Glenn said.

Blaine looked so still, so pale and small. Terra felt really scared. What was happening?

One paramedic snapped some questions at them, but they didn't know many of the answers. "It was some sort of pills, that's all we know, we weren't there," Glenn told them.

The paramedic eyed them dubiously but didn't say any more.

*　　*　　*

At the hospital, the paramedics rushed down the hall with the stretcher. "You can wait there." One pointed to a few chairs clustered at the end of the hallway.

Terra sank into one of the chairs, staring at a crack in the linoleum floor. "Hey," said Glenn. "Are you okay?"

She shook her head, the tears brimming over her eyelids again. "I shouldn't have just stopped hanging out with Blaine, I should have tried to get her to stop drugs. That's what a real friend would have done."

"Oh, Terra." Glenn sat down beside her and touched the back of her hand. "Blaine's a smart girl. She knew drugs can be dangerous. Everyone has to make their own decisions."

"But I should have at least tried."

Glenn took her hand and squeezed it. He patted her awkwardly on the arm. "Listen, the nurse told me they'll contact Blaine's mom. But I'm going to call my grandparents. I think you should call your parents too; they'll be wondering where you are."

He put some change into her hand, and robot-like, she crossed over to the payphone, put in the money and dialled home. "Mom..." she said, and promptly burst out crying. "No, no, I'm okay..."

"Here," said Glenn, gently taking the phone from her. "Mrs. Morrison? Hi. This is Terra's friend Glenn. We're at the hospital. No, no...we're perfectly fine. It's Terra's friend Blaine, she's collapsed, and we came along with her in the ambulance."

He handed the phone back to her. "Terra?" said her mother. "We'll come meet you there."

As she hung up the phone, a tall, dark-haired woman rushed past, calling Blaine's name. A nurse quickly took her by the arm and led her down the hall.

Terra and Glenn sat down in the waiting room again.

The fluorescent lights seemed really bright, and Terra found herself fixated by the reflected glare on the floor tiles. They glistened, freshly washed. A small plastic sign sat in the middle of the floor: "Caution, Wet." There was a picture of a little stick man, slipping. Terra wondered how often that actually happened. Of course, falling in a hospital was probably as good a place as any. Despite everything, she smiled to herself.

"What?" said Glenn.

She blushed, realizing he'd been watching her closely. "Nothing."

Just then, her parents and Glenn's grandfather arrived at almost exactly the same time. "Why, hello Grandpa Bob," said Terra's mom. "This is my husband, Duncan."

"Hello, Sharon." The two men shook hands. "Nice to meet you, Duncan," said Grandpa Bob. "Have you met my grandson, Glenn?"

Glenn stood up and solemnly shook hands with Terra's father. "I didn't think it would be at the hospital, but it's nice to meet you, sir."

"Okay," said Grandpa Bob, settling tentatively into a half-broken hospital chair. "Tell us what happened, Glenn."

Glenn quietly told everyone exactly what had happened.

"Drugs?" said Terra's mom. She sounded horrified. "Are you guys taking drugs?"

"Sharon," said Terra's father, putting his arm around her. "Just stay calm."

He took a deep breath and looked seriously at Terra. "Are you guys taking drugs?"

"No!" protested Terra.

"Honestly, no," added Glenn, "we just came to help Blaine."

"Glenn knows to stay away from drugs," said Grandpa Bob. Then he frowned. "The other kids just ran away?"

Glenn nodded. "I think they didn't want to get in trouble."

"Still!" protested Terra's mom. "What kind of friends are those? She's lucky you two were around."

They all sat silently for a moment. Grandpa Bob appeared to be praying.

Terra's mother squeezed her hand and smiled at her.

"Excuse me, miss," Grandpa Bob halted a nurse as she rushed by. "A young girl was brought in by ambulance—Blaine—can you tell us how she's doing?"

"Are you relations?"

"No. But these kids are her friends; they found her and called the ambulance."

"Just a moment." She disappeared through a set of swinging doors.

A moment later, she was back. "Okay, they took her to have her stomach pumped. But it looks like she's going to be okay. I should be able to tell you more in a little while."

Terra felt the tightness in her chest relax a little.

But just then a police officer walked down the hall, over to where Terra and Glenn sat. "Are you the kids that rode in with Blaine?"

"Yes, sir," said Glenn.

"Can you tell me what happened?"

Glenn repeated the story again.

"Hmm," said the officer, peering at them. "And you say you weren't doing any drugs yourselves?"

They shook their heads. Terra felt nervous to have the police asking her questions like that, even though she knew she hadn't done anything wrong.

"Definitely not," said Glenn, firmly.

The officer nodded. "Do you know who might have provided the drugs?"

Terra looked at Glenn.

"Yeah," he said, without hesitation. "Pete Reilly."

"Do you know where he lives?"

"Sorta." Glenn gave him a location.

The officer scribbled that down, then closed his notebook. He stood up. "Okay. Well, stay out of trouble."

It seemed like a moment out of a commercial or a bad TV show. Terra didn't know whether to laugh or cry.

But Glenn just nodded calmly. "For sure."

The nurse returned. "She's awake. I told her you were here. You can see her, for a moment. Her mother's with her now."

Terra's mom squeezed her hand, to get her attention.

"Oh!" Terra jumped up. She turned to Glenn. "Are you coming?"

He shook his head. "You go."

Terra followed the nurse down the hall.

In the room, Blaine's mother jumped up and gave Terra a hug. "Thanks for getting her to the hospital."

Blaine lay white-faced on the bed. She was attached to an IV. "It's just saline," she said, hoarsely. "They thought I needed some fluids."

"Oh," said Terra. She wasn't sure what else to say. She laid her hand carefully over Blaine's—the one that didn't have the needle protruding from it. "Are you okay?"

"I feel like..." Blaine glanced over at her mother, "Doggie do-do."

"Ah. Yeah… I'm not surprised to hear it. You really scared us."

Blaine frowned slightly. "How did you get here?"

Terra briefly described how Paula had called to them in the park, and how Glenn had phoned for an ambulance.

"Where's Paula?" Blaine craned her neck towards the door of the hospital room.

"Oh," said Terra, distressed. She glanced at Blaine's

mother. Finally, she just blurted out the truth. "Well, she left when we heard the sirens."

"And Pete?" Blaine looked like she was about to cry.

"He left too," Terra whispered.

"Figures," said Blaine bitterly. She laid her head back against the pillow.

"I told you he was no good," said Blaine's mother.

Blaine closed her eyes and didn't bother to answer.

"Terra," whispered the nurse. "Blaine needs to sleep now." The nurse guided her back towards the waiting room.

"She's going to be just fine," said the nurse. "But there's nothing more you can do here right now, you should probably head on home."

They said goodbye to Glenn and Grandpa Bob, and Terra walked to the car with her parents. To her surprise, her mom suddenly gave her a hug, then her dad kissed her forehead.

They got in the car, and nobody said anything for the whole drive home.

Dear Diary:

What a very strange, unbelievable day.

The scariest part of it all is, I know that could have easily been me, in that hospital bed—if things had gone just a little differently.

eleven

"T erra," her dad said tentatively, over the dinner table. He speared a piece of potato and sat there holding it. He was staring at her intently with his eyebrows drawn together.

"Hmm?" she shifted, uncomfortable under the unusual scrutiny.

"You *don't* do drugs, do you?"

"What? No!"

"Are you sure?"

"Yes!"

"Oh." He lifted the potato to his mouth, then paused. "Yes, you're sure you don't take drugs, or yes, you do take drugs?"

"Dad!" Terra was exasperated. "I don't take drugs!" She frowned at him.

"Uh. Good…don't start, okay?"

She sighed and nodded. "Of course not."

"What about that boy? Glenn?"

"What about him?"

"Does he do drugs?"

"No. He hates drugs."

"Ah. Well. Good." He resumed eating.

Terra sat there, looking at the now-chilled meatloaf and potatoes. "Dad?" she ventured, softly.

"Hmm?"

"I tried smoking though," she almost whispered the admission.

She heard her mother gasp.

"Oh…" Her father laid down his fork and looked at her seriously.

Terra swallowed, and they all sat silently for a moment.

"How was that?" he asked finally.

"I didn't really like it."

"Ah," said her father. He slowly ate another potato. "Are you going to smoke again?"

Terra shook her head. "No."

"Why not?"

"Because… it's not that fun, and it's smelly, and they're expensive and illegal for kids to buy. And…" Terra hesitated.

"And?" her father asked mildly.

She stared down at the table. "And…Glenn doesn't like it."

"Ah," was all he said. He glanced quickly at his wife.

Her mother cleared her throat. "More milk, Terra?"

*   *   *

"So," said Terra, sitting in the library at a small study table, across from Tracy. The light from a nearby window streamed over and through the bookcases, creating interesting patterns of shadow on the tabletop.

"Yeah. So." Tracy idly traced her fingertip along a shadow mark.

They looked at each other blankly, then at the equally blank pieces of paper in front of them.

"Well," said Tracy, picking up her pencil and gripping it firmly.

"Yeah," nodded Terra. They looked at each other, then burst out giggling. The librarian frowned at them. They giggled some more, but more quietly.

"We really have to get working on this history project."

"Yeah," agreed Tracy amicably. She leaned back in her chair, letting her head fall over the back, her arms dangling at her sides. "I found some books that should help, very heavy books." She lifted one hand and pointed weakly at the stack beside her.

"Cool. I found some stuff on the Internet that should help us—from the National Archives. Actually, it's kind of an interesting topic—when women became 'persons.'"

Tracy shook her head. "I can't believe women were ever not considered persons!"

"It's true though. Women couldn't sit in the Canadian senate—they weren't considered persons under the law. It wasn't that long ago, either." Terra opened her textbook. "Yeah, see? Not even a hundred years ago—1928—the Supreme Court said women weren't 'persons' who could hold office as senators."

Tracy frowned. "That's ridiculous." But she scribbled down the date. "When did it change?"

"Hmm. The next year, I think. It all had to do with a group of women appealing the 'persons' case."

"Oh, yeah. I saw something about that." Tracy flipped through one of the big books in front of her. "That was the 'The Famous Five'—Nellie McClung, Louise McKinney, Henrietta Muir Edwards, Emily Murphy and Irene Parlby."

"Hmm. I've heard of some of those names, I think. Especially Nellie McClung."

"Yeah," Tracy turned the page. "She was involved in getting women the right to vote."

"When did that happen?"

"Well, it was 1916 at the federal level. Oh, and Nellie McClung was a member of the provincial legislature in Alberta, from 1921 to 1926."

"Wow." Terra rubbed the sides of her forehead. "It's hard to imagine that women couldn't vote. That's insane."

Tracy made a face. "Well, we don't get to vote either. That's not fair."

"Yeah, because we're too young. But at least it's the same for the guys. They can't vote either until they're eighteen."

Tracy grimaced. "I think girls should be able to vote earlier. Everyone says girls mature faster."

"Hee." Terra laughed. "So who do you want to vote for?"

Tracy blinked. "Oh, I dunno! I'd have to look into it for a bit."

Terra nodded. "You've got four years to look into it."

"Very funny," Tracy mumbled. But she smiled at Terra, and both girls continued making notes.

*　　*　　*

Terra called Blaine's house after school. The phone rang several times, as if the answering machine was turned off. She wondered if she should let it ring a few more times or just give up. Just when she was about to put down the phone, a tired-sounding voice answered, "Hello?"

It was Blaine's mother. She told Terra that Blaine was now home from the hospital, but she was sleeping and couldn't come to the phone.

"Oh," said Terra hastily. "That's okay. I just wanted to say hello and see how she was doing."

"Yeah," said Blaine's mom. "We're hanging in there. I'll tell her you called."

"Okay. Thanks."

"Uh, Terra?"

"Yes?'

"Thanks for being a good friend to her. And sorry if I was a bit weird at the hospital. I wasn't sure if you were one of her druggie friends or not."

"Oh," said Terra, uncertain what to say to that.

"But Blaine told me the whole story, as much as she remembered, anyhow."

"Oh."

"Well, thanks again. I'll tell her you called."

*   *   *

Two days later, Blaine was back at school. Terra saw her in the hall, just before second period.

She wanted to rush over, but she held back for a moment, not wanting to make a big deal of seeing her back at school, in case Blaine didn't want that. Their eyes met. Blaine hesitated, nodded, then turned on her heel and slipped back into the crowd.

With a hollow feeling in her chest, Terra almost felt like crying. Even after everything that had happened, Blaine still didn't want to be friends?

"Hey," said Glenn softly, behind her shoulder. "You okay?"

"Yeah," swallowed Terra. "It's just...did you just see Blaine? It looked like she doesn't want to talk to me."

"Aw," said Glenn, tapping lightly on her locker. "She's probably just embarrassed, Terra. A lot of kids know what happened. It must be kind of hard—and you saw her at the worst—the part she can't even remember. And she's kind of proud, I think."

"Yeah…" Terra stared at her shoelace, which was half undone. She bent down and did it up, which gave her the chance to furtively wipe away a tear.

"Don't worry," said Glenn. "It's going to be okay."

"Yeah…" said Terra and closed her locker. It seemed to stick, so she put her hip into it and gave it an extra shove. The locker banged loudly as it snapped in place.

* * *

Working on the history project with Tracy was a lot of fun. Whatever hesitations Tracy had initially had about extending friendship to Terra seemed to have disappeared. Instead, she now went out of her way to include her in discussions and activities.

"You showed her you wanted to be her friend too," Winter noted quietly to Terra. "She's got a tendency to be possessive, especially about her friendship with Kaitlin. You showed her you were interested in being her friend too, not just Kaitlin's."

"Um…"

"So, uh, good job," grinned Winter.

Terra frowned, uncertain whether Winter was making fun of her. But Winter just gave a wave and headed off to class.

* * *

The day they were to make their presentations to the class, Tracy showed up at Terra's locker with a large shopping bag. She pulled out two black satin jackets, embroidered with pink lettering on the back, proclaiming: "I'M A PERSON TOO."

Terra couldn't stop laughing as they tried them on. "These are great, Tracy! Wow!"

Tracy smiled demurely. "Thanks. My mom got them for us."

Kaitlin shrieked and came running across the hall to look as the girls modelled the jackets.

"Oh man, those are fab-u-lous," drawled Winter.

"Oh WOman, don't you mean?" joked Kaitlin, poking Winter lightly in the ribs.

Everybody laughed. "I do stand corrected!" Winter grinned.

Tracy and Terra headed off to class and waited for their turn to present.

They were a little nervous, but after a bit of a stammering start and a few giggles, it went very well. Best of all, just before class was over, the teacher handed them each a note. "Good job, persons! A+!"

* * *

Terra proudly wore her persons jacket the rest of the day.

"You're a person?" Glenn queried, squinting at the jacket.

"Yep." She grinned at him and almost skipped along the hall—the adrenalin was still flowing from the success of the presentation.

"I don't get it. Did somebody say you weren't?"

"Yeah." Terra laughed. "The Supreme Court!"

His eyebrows furrowed together. "Okay, I really don't get it."

"You shoulda been in our history class." She tossed him a small file. "Here's our project—feel free to educate yourself." She smiled sweetly at him.

He looked down at the stack of papers. "I guess I walked into that one."

"Yeah. Still, it's kind of interesting."

"I'll read it, don't worry." He fell into step beside her. "So, it looks like you and Tracy are getting along okay now?"

She nodded. "Yeah. And you know, I really do like her."

"That's cool." He paused for a moment. "You know, I really like you."

"You're just saying that."

"Why would I just be saying that?"

"Because…" Terra searched her mind for something light. "Because—I'm a person!"

Smiling, he moved his face closer to hers.

Terra felt her heart stop and her stomach clench into a knot. "So, um…don't forget to read this." She tapped the edge of her paper, then she walked quickly away.

*   *   *

"Nice jacket," said a quiet voice behind her.

Terra sprang around to see Blaine standing there. "Oh…hi."

"Hey."

The two girls looked at each other for a moment.

"It's to do with history class," Terra blurted out. "When the Supreme Court said the word persons didn't apply to women."

"Yeah. That sucked. Good thing they figured it out."

"Yeah."

Blaine cleared her throat. "So, uh, I guess I should say thank you, for taking care of me and calling an ambulance and all that."

"Well, it was actually Glenn who called. He has a cell phone."

Blaine shrugged. "Yeah. But…you know."

"Okay." Terra nodded. "It's okay. You're welcome."

They both stood there awkwardly.

"Did you hear that Pete got arrested?"

"Wow. Really?"

"Yeah. Apparently the police showed up at his place with a search warrant and found some drugs and stuff, and he's in pretty big trouble."

"Oh." Terra didn't know what to say about that. "Are you upset? Because he's your boyfriend?"

Blaine tossed her hair. "He's not my boyfriend after ditching me like that. And I've got no use for that Paula either. "

"I think she was pretty upset though."

"Yeah? Not enough to stick around, eh? I don't want anything to do with her."

"Oh," said Terra. "I'm sorry. I know they were your friends."

Blaine shrugged with deliberate nonchalance. "I guess I don't need any friends."

They were quiet for a moment.

"What about me?" Terra almost whispered. "I'm your friend."

Blaine suddenly appeared shy. "Yeah?"

"Yeah," said Terra firmly.

"Cool," said Blaine. Then in an undertone, with a slight smile: "Don't make me wear some matching 'person' coat, though."

Terra burst out laughing. "It's a deal."

"Hey, Terra!" yelled Kaitlin across the hallway. "What are you doing? We're going to stop and see Grandma Lorna after school. Do you want to come?"

"Oh. Are we invited?"

With a small laugh, Winter shrugged her coat on. "She told us it was a standing invitation! We drop by after school every now and then. Don't worry, it's cool." She turned to

Blaine. "Hi, Blaine. Why don't you come too?"

Blaine seemed startled. "Uh…what?"

"Come visit Grandma Lorna," urged Kaitlin.

"Uh…who?"

"Does Glenn know you're coming?" Terra interrupted.

Kaitlin shrugged. "I doubt it. But it doesn't matter. We're not going to visit Glenn. We're going to visit Grandma Lorna!"

"Um. Well, I'd have to call my mom."

"Here," piped in Tracy helpfully. "Use my cell phone. You too, Blaine."

"Uh…" squirmed Blaine.

Terra expected her mother to ask a lot of pointed questions. Surprisingly, she didn't. "The girls are visiting Grandma Lorna? Okay. Have a good time, dear."

Terra stared at the phone for a moment, then handed it back to Tracy. "Well. She said it's okay."

Kaitlin let out a cheer.

"Oh, good. Would you like to call your mother too, Blaine?" Tracy offered politely.

Blaine shifted from one foot to the other. She looked to Terra, who smiled encouragingly at her. "Well. I probably should. She's protective these days."

Everyone nodded, but no one commented.

The talk about the incident in the park and the ambulance had spread really quickly. Still, no one here was bringing it up.

Terra watched her new friends reach out to include Blaine, and she felt a warm sensation spread in her chest.

"Hey, Ma," said Blaine quietly. "I'm just going out for a bit to visit somebody's grandma with some girls from school…yeah, yeah, Terra's going too. Okay, okay, bye."

She made a pained face. "If you're going, Terra, it's okay."

"Yay, yay, everybody's coming!" Kaitlin and Tracy linked arms and did a little dance in the hall.

"Grand," Winter declared. "So…let's go!"

The girls—Kaitlin, Winter, Tracy, Blaine and Terra—strode down the sidewalk in a group, talking and laughing. Terra was surprised to realize how comfortable she felt with these girls—almost like they were her friends and she belonged. Wow.

"Hey," Tracy nudged her. "What's up? You're awfully quiet."

Terra smiled. "I was just thinking, I guess."

"What!" protested Kaitlin. "There will be no thinking!"

Winter rolled her eyes.

*   *   *

Grandma Lorna answered the door with a big smile on her face. "Hello, girls!"

Even though she looked pleased to see them, she didn't seem particularly surprised. "You're just in time for a batch of chocolate chip cookies I made especially for you!"

"But you didn't know we were coming!" Tracy protested.

She chuckled. "I get feelings about such things."

"Awesome," beamed Winter, as the girls piled inside. She introduced Blaine.

"Oh, wonderful. It's so nice to meet you, Blaine," said Grandma Lorna. "And it's nice to see you too, Terra! Won't Glenn be surprised!"

Tracy giggled and poked Terra, who felt her face growing warm.

"It's nice to see you too," she said. What will Glenn think, Terra thought to herself—finding me eating cookies in his kitchen?

"Those are nice jackets, girls," said Grandma Lorna, peering at them over her glasses.

"Thanks. My mom made them up for a history presentation we did," said Tracy, her mouth full of cookie. "We got an A!"

"Wonderful! About the 'persons' case, I presume."

Terra looked up, surprised. "You remember that?"

"My dear, I'm not that old."

"Oh." Terra blushed deeply. "I didn't mean…"

"Do I remember learning about it? Yes, I do. But to be honest, I had a bit of refresher, since Glenn brought home your paper on it at lunch."

Terra felt oddly embarrassed, but Grandma Lorna just smiled at her. "Good job, girls."

"Thanks!" munched Tracy.

"It's really quite something, the advances that have been made for women's rights, in a relatively short time," commented Grandma Lorna.

"Girls can do whatever they want, whatever boys can do," interjected Tracy.

"Yes, that's what I mean. It's amazing to me that girls and women of your generation don't even hesitate to pursue your dreams, and feel that everything's open to you. I think that's great."

Kaitlin frowned slightly. "But hasn't it been like that for awhile? I mean, Jane, my mom, is a lawyer."

"Yes, and that's great. But I bet if you ask them, that even your mothers will have faced discrimination of some sort because they're women. Anyhow, ask them about it." She poured them all a glass of milk to go with the cookies.

"So what do you girls want to be after school?"

"When we grow up…" Tracy mumbled with her mouth full of crumbs.

"Hmm…I'm thinking I'd like to be a doctor," said Kaitlin.

"A family doctor?"

"Well…" Kaitlin hesitated. "I'm thinking about being an oncologist, to try and help people with cancer, like my mother."

"Not Jane," whispered Tracy, to Terra and Blaine, "her first mother."

"I used to always say I wanted to be an astronaut, but I don't really know," Winter admitted.

"I don't know either," said Terra.

Tracy shook her head and shrugged.

"That's okay. You girls still have lots of time to make those decisions."

"I'd like to be a journalist," Blaine offered shyly. "I think it would be neat to write for a newspaper, about politics or new discoveries or whatever."

"Yeah," said Tracy. "It would be fun to be on the news."

"In a trench coat, clutching a microphone, with the wind blowing your hair all around," suggested Kaitlin. "Yeah, that would be cool!"

Everybody laughed.

Just then, Glenn walked in. He didn't seem surprised to find his kitchen full of females, but he paused when he saw Terra. His gaze travelled to Blaine, and he smiled.

"Hi, girls," he said.

"We ate all your cookies, Glenn!" Kaitlin called out cheerily.

"What?" he asked, clutching his chest, pretending to be in shock.

"Now, now," Grandma Lorna laughed. "You know me better than that." She went over to the counter and came back a moment later with another plateful of cookies.

"Thanks, Grandma," said Glenn, giving her a kiss on the cheek. "You're the best!"

When Kaitlin announced she had to get home, everyone else got up too. Grandma Lorna saw them to the door and told them to come back again soon.

"Wow," said Blaine to Terra when they reached the sidewalk. "Milk and cookies and grandmas aren't really my thing…but that was kinda okay, wasn't it?"

Terra smiled and nodded. "Yeah. It really was."

She waved as Blaine turned off in the direction of her house.

"May I walk with you?" asked Glenn, shrugging into a jean jacket as he ran down the steps.

"Sure," Terra nodded.

They stopped at the small park near Terra's house. The wind was picking up, and she could feel it tossing her hair about. She paused for a moment and refastened the clip to keep it out of her eyes.

A few little kids were running around a set of monkeybars, shrieking. That made Terra smile. She remembered how she'd liked to climb them too, when she was little. One small boy just kept running around in circles.

Glenn noticed the direction of Terra's gaze. "So, you want to do some climbing?"

She blinked. "What?"

"Come on. They'll still hold you!"

"I wasn't worried about that!" she protested. "It's just that we're too old for monkeybars!"

"Bah. You're only as old as you feel. Isn't that what they say?"

"I guess. But it doesn't really make sense, does it? After all, you're as old as you actually are, not as old as you feel, right?"

He laughed and shook his head. "You think too much! Come on!" He pulled her by the arm and gave her a little push until she started to climb up the structure. It felt strange to do something like this, after so many years. One of the little kids paused underneath to stare at her for a moment, then he kept on with his running in circles.

Glenn dashed around to the other side of the monkey bars and climbed up to join Terra at the top.

"It's really high! I mean, a little kid could hurt themselves, falling from here."

"Well, there's sand down below."

"Still. I wouldn't want to fall from here."

He laughed and put a hand over hers for a moment, on the bar. "Don't worry, Terra. I won't let you fall."

She felt a weird feeling in her stomach. "Don't look at me like that."

"Like what?" he blinked at her curiously.

"Like that!" She pointed at him.

"Hmm," he said. "Okay. So…why not?"

"Well," she glanced at him, and then blurted out honestly: "It makes me feel ill!"

"What!" The amused expression dropped off Glenn's face. "What do you mean?"

"Oh." She hastened to make it sound better. "I mean, sometimes you make me nervous, and I have a nervous stomach. So, if I'm nervous, I feel like I'm going to throw up."

"Like that time you threw up in the park?"

She blushed deeply, but nodded. "Yeah, like that."

He shook his head. He reached out, as if he was going to pat her hand, but then withdrew his own, as if he thought better of it. "Seriously, though, Terra. You don't have to be nervous of me. I just want to spend time with you and get to know you. That's not scary, is it?"

She paused, then answered honestly. "It's a bit scary."

"It is?"

He considered, then smiled. "Yeah, maybe a bit. Still, you don't want to throw up about that, do you?"

She shook her head ruefully. "No, no, I don't."

"Whew!" Glenn chuckled, and Terra laughed too. "So. We can just talk and get to know each other better. I bet there are a lot of things about you that I don't know."

A cloud passed over Terra's face. "Yeah. I guess you're right," she said glumly. "I should tell you."

"Hey. I didn't mean to pry or anything like that, Terra. You don't have to tell me anything you don't want to."

"No," she said resolutely. "I'll tell you."

Glenn looked a bit apprehensive as Terra took a deep breath. Then she blurted out: "I'm adopted!"

"Oh," said Glenn, finally.

Terra raised her head to look at him.

"You seemed so serious for a moment, I was worried you were about to confess to a crime or something."

"No," said Terra. "That's my big secret."

To her horror, the tears started to run down her cheeks. Within minutes, she'd told Glenn the whole story—about the photos and the letter, and about how she'd never signed the annual Christmas card.

"Why not?" asked Glenn. "Are you mad at her?"

She shrugged. "I don't know. I don't know how to feel about it."

"It's not that big a deal, is it? Being adopted?"

"It feels like a big deal."

"Yeah, I guess," he conceded. "But...you've got parents who love you, and that's really cool, isn't it?"

Terra remembered then that Glenn didn't live with his parents. "Yeah," she said, but glumly.

"Families these days are weird anyway, Terra. I live with

my grandparents. Kaitlin has a stepmother and half sister. You're adopted. So whatever. As long as you have people who really care about you, I think you're in pretty good shape."

Terra was unconvinced. "You won't tell anybody?" She felt a sense of panic that the word might get out.

"Of course not, it's your business. But I don't think anybody would think any differently of you if you did tell them. But I won't say anything."

He stood up, took her hand helped her down. He held her hand for just a moment at the bottom and smiled at her. "Let me walk you the rest of the way home?"

She nodded. "Sure."

When they got to her house, they paused at the end of the driveway. "Do you want to come in?" Terra asked shyly.

"Yeah! I was hoping you'd ask!"

They tripped over wood and construction materials on the way in.

"What's going on?" asked Glenn curiously.

"We're renovating," Terra sighed.

"Yes, isn't it great?" a deep voice inquired. Fred was suddenly behind them.

Glenn put out his hand and Fred pumped it enthusiastically, all the while looking him up and down.

"Um. Hi Fred. This is Glenn," said Terra.

"Nice to meet you, Glenn!"

"Nice to meet you too, sir."

They went into the living room. "Wow," said Glenn. "Nice piano! Is it okay if I play it?"

Terra blinked, surprised. "Sure. Do you know how?"

"Ah, just a bit. My Grandma teaches me. How about you?"

"No, I took a few years of lessons, but I hated to practice. My mom plays, though."

Glenn pushed back the lid and sat at the piano bench. He ran his fingers over the keys in a few scales. "Wow, nice sound." Then, to Terra's surprise, he broke into a jazz tune.

"That's amazing! Your grandmother taught you that?"

"Well. She taught me the basics, and some more traditional stuff, but lately I've been working on some improvisation."

"That's so cool. I had no idea you could do that."

"Yeah. See why we need to get to know each other?"

She blushed. "Play some more!"

He smiled and hit the keys again. Bending over them, he coaxed a rousing tune out of the instrument. When he finally brought it to an end, they heard loud applause right behind them.

Unnoticed, Fred and Terra's parents had come into the room to listen to the music.

"Oh!" Glenn looked embarrassed and jumped up, folding his hands behind his back.

"No, no, keep going!" her dad insisted.

"Aw, that's pretty much my whole repertoire."

"Well, I do hope you'll keep it up. It's a shame to let talent go to waste." Terra's mom looked pointedly at her.

Behind Glenn, Terra frowned, but he didn't notice.

"Thanks. I've been thinking about signing up for some formal lessons, but things are pretty busy, with school and basketball games and practice."

Her dad nodded. "Yeah. I guess you have to figure out which things you really want to make time for. But I hope that will include piano. You're pretty good."

"Thank you, sir," said Glenn.

"Would you guys like a snack or something?" asked her mother.

"Oh, no, thank you. My Grandma stuffed us with

cookies. I only hope I have a bit of room left for supper! Speaking of that, I'd better get going…"

*   *   *

She stood looking out the window, even after Glenn had disappeared from view.

"He seems like a nice kid," said her father.

"Yeah," said Terra.

Dear Diary:

My new friends are totally fun. And I really like Glenn; and it seems that he likes me too!

Plus, my parents are being cool.

Basically, everything is going okay for once.

So what's the deal?

twelve

As the janitor pushed his cart through the school, he left a floor smelling strongly of cleaner. The bell rang and the kids exploded out into the hall, parting in an uneven flood around the janitor's stuff.

Blaine stood with her hands on her hips, looking down the hall. "You're right, Terra."

Terra blinked. "Huh?"

"What are you right about?" inquired Winter airily.

"Uh....I dunno," Terra said.

Winter laughed. "Ah!"

"Terra says we should do something about Joyce's bullying."

Terra could feel furrows developing on her forehead.

"Um…I did?"

"Yeah, that's a good idea," said Kaitlin. "What did you have in mind, Terra?"

"I…uh…"

Blaine raised her fists. "We could make them really sorry."

"Well, I don't think…" interjected Terra.

"I'm with Terra on that," agreed Kaitlin. "That's not really my style. But there must be something we can do."

"Should we tell on them?" suggested Tracy.

"Hmm. I guess we could. But wouldn't it be kind of our

word against theirs? It would be better if we could have proof of some sort."

"Evidence…" pondered Winter.

"Oh, yeah, Winter will be able to think of something! Come on, Winter!" Kaitlin cheered.

Winter raised an eyebrow. "Well, here's just a thought…but maybe we could capture something on video…"

Kaitlin frowned, thinking. "We could borrow a digital video camera from the computer lab," she said.

"I'm not very good with computers, guys," Blaine noted.

"Don't worry, Winter is excellent at them."

"Uh, no pressure," muttered Winter, but she smiled at Blaine. "Yeah, it should be okay—we could probably make it work."

Terra felt the unseen hand already squeezing her stomach.

"This is going to be so cool," grinned Kaitlin.

"Very cool," said Tracy. "Good idea, Terra!"

"Umm…" sighed Terra. She shook her head and followed Blaine mutely to math class. Her stomach rolled warningly.

"Hey, Blaine," said Paula, in the hallway.

Blaine muttered something unintelligible and kept on walking.

Terra looked at Paula, but Paula was just staring sadly after Blaine.

*   *   *

"I think Paula must feel bad about what happened," said Terra to Blaine after class.

"Yeah. Maybe. That's what she keeps telling me."

"That she's sorry?"

"Yeah."

113

"You don't believe her?"

Blaine shrugged. "It's not that—I'm just trying to get things straightened out, and I don't think she's good for me. Do you know what I mean?"

Terra hesitated. "Do you mean that you're trying to figure out what kind of person you want to be, and you don't think Paula's helping you get there?"

Blaine just stared at her, and Terra felt her face start to redden.

But then Blaine gave a little smile and shrug. "Yeah, something like that. Not that I'd say it like that…"

"No, me neither."

"You just did!"

"Oh, yeah."

*   *   *

Terra rather hoped her new Inglewood friends had forgotten about Joyce and her bullying. But it wasn't to be.

Instead, it seemed that once the girls had a project in mind, they took it seriously.

First, Winter signed out a notebook computer and a video camera from the school resource centre. Then Kaitlin got herself excused from class early before lunch, and managed to place the camera inconspicuously on top of the lockers, near where Joyce and her gang tended to hang out.

Thanks to the school's new wireless network, the girls were able to huddle in the library around the computer and wait.

Sure enough, Joyce and her friends showed up, crowding around a small blonde girl. In remarkable clarity, the video showed her hand over money, before the bigger girls moved away.

The camera captured the tears rolling down the girl's cheek, and Joyce's laughter. Then the girls moved on to their next victim.

"Wow," said Blaine, making a fist. "Are you sure you don't just want to deal with this ourselves?"

"No, no, no…this is much better," said Kaitlin. "So who wants to go get the camera? We can't leave it there." She turned around and looked at Terra, her eyebrow raised questioningly.

"Well," protested Terra. She scrutinized the computer screen. The girls seemed to have vacated the area.

"Great," Kaitlin grinned. "Just grab the camera and meet us back here."

"I don't like this…" said Terra. However, her rubber legs seemed to be carrying her out of the library. Somehow, she walked down the hall, trying to look nonchalant. Until she saw Joyce and her friends, that is.

They scowled at her and said nothing until she was past them, but even that indistinguishable murmur sent little chills up Terra's spine. Somehow, those kids were excellent at intimidation, she thought.

She walked to the end of the hall and casually reached up to the top of the locker to grab the camera. She tried to make it look like she was just stretching. She dropped the small camera into her pocket.

"Hey!" called Joyce challengingly.

Terra felt herself succumb to a small heart attack.

"Get away from my locker." The bigger girl scowled at her.

"Uh, sorry." Terra slowly moved away. Walking down the hall, she glanced backwards once, to see Joyce standing there with her hands on her hips staring after her.

She ran into the library and thrust the camera at Winter.

"Here!" she gasped.

The other girls eyed her curiously. "There, there," said Kaitlin and patted her on the back. "A stupendous effort, my dear."

"Yes," agreed Winter smoothly, "a momentous contribution."

Tracy giggled.

Terra sank down in a chair and buried her face in her arms at the table, moaning.

Winter turned her attention back to the computer screen. "I've set up an anonymous email address, and I'm going to send a clip of the video to the principal's office."

"Shouldn't you write a note too?" queried Tracy.

"Yeah, I guess so. Hmm…" Winter contemplated the blank screen, then started to type.

Dear Principal's Office:
    Please view the enclosed video for proof that there's unacceptable bullying going on in this school.
    We trust you will take appropriate action against the perpetrators.
    Yours truly,
    Some Concerned Citizens

Terra lifted her head from the table opened one eye and viewed the short letter. She moaned again.

"Oh, that's good!" exclaimed Kaitlin. "I think that's just right."

"Yeah, cool," agreed Blaine.

Winter merely smiled. She attached the video clip to the email and hit "send".

Tracy frowned, but she was looking at Terra. "What's wrong? You don't look so good, Terra. Do you feel like you're going to throw up?"

"Uh, yeah, I think I might."

The other girls laughed sympathetically.

*   *   *

Later, everybody was talking about how Joyce and her friends had been called out of class by Mr. Brenner, the vice-principal.

Everyone seemed to have a different story or speculation about what was going on. Terra and her friends just kept their heads down and said nothing, but Kaitlin was grinning broadly.

When she had to pass the principal's office between classes, Terra walked very fast. But she noticed someone had further vandalized the sign. Instead of saying Poffice, it had been edited—and now said POLLICE.

Dear Diary:

Have you ever noticed—sometimes doing the right thing is very stressful too?

Who would have thought it?

thirteen

W"ow," said Terra, staring out over the blue-green water of Lake Louise. The mountains towered all around.

"Isn't the scenery just stunning out here?" whispered her mother. "I'm so glad we made the drive."

Terra nodded—she couldn't help herself. "Yeah…"

"The mountains are magnificent," said her father. "You just have to be amazed by God's creation, when you see a place like this."

Terra squinted up at the sky.

It really is beautiful, she thought to herself. But then she felt a bit disloyal. "It doesn't have the nice fall colours though, like at home."

"True," her dad conceded. "We're not seeing the reds and oranges we're used to from Ontario's maple trees."

Her mother smiled. "Each place is special in its own way. Come on, Terra. Help me with our picnic lunch."

Later, they climbed up a rocky path to get a higher viewpoint. Her parents were moving quickly, and Terra could feel her heart rate pick up as she scrambled over the small rocks.

Ahead, her father helped pull her mother up onto a large rock, where they stood, overlooking the valley. As Terra approached, her dad, and then her mom, both reached down to give her a hand. They tugged her up but didn't immediately let go.

But Terra didn't pull away either. After all, it wasn't like her friends could see.

Her mom smiled at her. "I'm glad you came out with us today."

"Yeah, yeah," Terra mumbled.

But she smiled too.

*   *   *

"Whoa," said her father, pressing rather heavily on the brake. Terra had been half-dozing in the backseat.

"Wha..?" she asked, sleepily.

"Look, Terra," whispered her mother.

Just in front of the car, a black bear stepped onto the road. It paused and looked at them, then slowly crossed the highway.

"Wow," said her dad, slowly stepping on the gas again. "You don't see that everyday."

Terra twisted in her seat, craning her neck, watching as the bear lumbered off into the trees.

*   *   *

The two girls ran down the steps on their way out of school, but Blaine suddenly stopped short.

Surprised, Terra almost ran into her.

Pete was standing at the bottom of the stairs, leaning against the railings, smoking a cigarette.

"Hey, Blaine." He ignored Terra but gave Blaine a casual smile.

She scowled. "I thought you were in jail."

He looked a bit embarrassed. "I'm waiting for my trial," he muttered.

"Huh. So...what do you want?"

He dropped the cigarette and stubbed it out with the toe of his boot. He gave her an appraising look. "Heh. Well...a little kiss might be nice."

Terra felt uncomfortable. Should she go or stay? She slowly took a half-step sideways.

Blaine's hand shot out and grabbed her arm, in a vice-grip. "Stay."

"Okay," whispered Terra.

"You've got to be kidding," Blaine told Pete. "You left me in that shack."

"Aw. I stayed until I heard the sirens."

"Yeah? My real friends stayed with me all the way to the hospital."

He looked a bit uncomfortable. "Yeah, well. Sorry 'bout that. I'll make it up to you."

She shook her head. "I don't think so."

"Aw, Blaine…"

"Get lost, Pete."

She walked away, with her chin up.

"Aw...come on, Blaine," he called.

Terra stared after her for a moment, then scrambled past Pete to catch up with her.

"Blaine!" he shouted, but they didn't look back. Terra held her breath, afraid he would run after them, but he didn't.

The two girls crossed the street and went into the park. They found a quiet spot and sat down in the grass.

"Wow, Blaine," Terra whispered. "I wish I had your nerve. You're so cool."

"Ya think so?" replied Blaine dryly.

Then to Terra's surprise, a tear rolled down Blaine's cheek. She wiped at it with the back of her hand, muttering.

"Oh," said Terra, "It's okay." She leaned forward and gave Blaine a hug. Right away, she knew she'd made a mistake, as the other girl stiffened, uncomfortably.

But then Blaine relaxed and hugged her back. "Okay, enough, enough…" Blaine was smiling, although her eyes were moist. "You're such a girl." She grinned.

Terra lifted her chin challengingly. "Yeah? What's wrong with that?"

"Nothing," said Blaine. "Not a thing."

*   *   *

"Heya Fred," said Terra, strolling up the front driveway to her house. He was lugging a toolbox out to his truck. "Are you finished?"

He rested the box on the asphalt and smiled at her. "Hi, Terra. Just for today. You didn't think I'd be leaving you so quickly, did you?"

She laughed. "Actually, no!"

"So how's your young man?"

"Glenn? Well, he's not really my young man."

"Anyway," he continued. "So how is he?"

Terra smiled shyly. "Aw, he's good."

"Well, that's all right then." He chuckled. "See you tomorrow, Terra!" He hefted up the toolbox and threw it into the back of the truck.

"Bye, Fred." Terra ran up the front steps into her house. Her mom and dad were sitting at the kitchen table with serious expressions on their faces.

"Hi, Terra," said her father.

"How was your day, dear?" said her mother.

"Um. Okay, thanks. Uh…how was yours?"

"Fine. Fine." They both nodded and looked at each other. "Fine, fine."

"I'm finally getting some interest from potential PR clients," volunteered her mom.

"Oh? Well, that's good."

Terra looked at her father.

"Well, they put the plaque with my name on the door today."

"That's probably a good sign?"

"Oh!" said her mom. "A double entendre!"

Terra blinked. "What? Oh yeah—a sign…heh." She smiled at them and turned to start up to her room.

"Uh, Terra," said her dad.

"Yes?"

He looked at her mother, who said, "We've had a letter from Donna."

"Who?" Terra asked unnecessarily. "Your birthmother, Terra," her mom explained patiently. "Would you like to read it?"

"No," said Terra, automatically and turned again towards the door.

"Terra." Her mom's voice was very soft. "She's coming through town for work—she lives in Vancouver now—and she's asked to meet you."

She stared at them. Her heart was beating very fast. "No. No, I don't want to."

Her father nodded. "You don't have to."

She felt her pulse slow slightly. "I don't want to."

"I was thinking you're probably a bit curious," her mother offered. "That would be a normal thing…"

"No," said Terra. "I'm not curious." Terra could feel the tears pricking at the back of her eyelids.

"All right, sweetie. But if you change your mind in the next few days, you just say so, okay?"

Terra shook her head. "I don't want to meet her," she repeated stubbornly.

"It's okay, Terra," her dad said.

She ran from the room and upstairs to her bedroom. She threw herself on the bed and sobbed into the pillow.

"Oh, honey," said her mom, a few moments later. She came into the room and sat down on the edge of Terra's bed. She gently rubbed Terra's back. "Don't cry."

"I'm not crying," Terra hiccupped.

Her mom paused. "My mistake."

But she still rubbed Terra's back. "Sweetie, you know that your dad and I love you very much. That you're our daughter, and you always will be? Nothing will change that."

Terra nodded into the pillow, sniffled. She lifted her head. "Are you sure, Mom?"

Her mom smiled at her, then hugged her very tightly. "Yeah, Terra. I'm really, really sure."

*   *   *

"Donna wants to meet me," Terra blurted out the next day.

Glenn rubbed his head. "Who?"

"My birthmother," she said impatiently. "Remember I told you about that?"

"Oh yeah, yeah, I remember. Sorry, I don't think I knew her name."

"So what do you think I should do?"

Glenn rubbed his head again. "What do you want to do?"

"I don't want to see her," said Terra.

He nodded. "Huh. So why are you asking, if you've made up your mind?"

"I don't know."

"Hmm."

"I guess I just want to be sure I'm making the right decision."

"Ah."

She gave him her most pathetic look. "Say something..."

"Oh, man," said Glenn. "I'm really bad at this kind of thing."

"What kind of thing?"

"Oh, advice, I guess. It's hard for me to know what to tell you. I think I should probably tell you to meet with her, but then I think about how angry I've been at my own dad—for leaving me and Mom, and I'm not sure what I'd do if he showed up wanting to see me. Then again," he smiled ruefully, "there's not much chance of that, so maybe I'm a bit jealous!" He paused. "Maybe you should meet her. After all...your mother...wow."

"She's NOT my mother!"

He frowned, nodded. "Yeah. Sorry. I mean—there's a biological connection there. That's got to be significant, somehow? Isn't it?"

"I don't know."

He sighed. "Maybe you should talk to the girls. Aren't girls supposed to be better at this sort of stuff?"

"What stuff?"

"Oh, the touchy-feely relationship stuff."

Terra poked him in the arm, not gently.

"Ouch!" He rubbed his arm. "Okay, sorry, sorry. But really, I don't think you should be shy to talk to them."

"But you think I should meet her?"

"I guess so, yeah. But it's up to you, not me."

She sighed, staring at the worn-out toe of her running shoe. "Yeah."

Walking home, Terra was lost in her own thoughts, some about Glenn, a whole lot about Donna. Suddenly a dark shadow fell across her path, and she looked up.

"Look who we have here," said Joyce smugly, backed up by two of her henchwomen. Terra was struck by the thought that Joyce was really very large, especially when she stood there, in the middle of the sidewalk, with her hands on her hips.

"If it isn't the tattle-tale," she continued. "Did you know we got suspended?!"

"I...um...yeah, I heard something about it," answered Terra, cautiously. After all, the news was pretty much the talk of the school the past week.

"Do you know why?

"Um...wasn't it for...bullying?"

"We got suspended," said Joyce, frowning, "because...some sneaky person took a video of us! So I thought about it—and who do I remember hanging around my locker? Well, I saw you there, didn't I?"

She took a step closer to Terra.

Terra stepped back.

Joyce laughed, humourlessly. "You're a real girl, aren't you?"

"Uh...yeah," said Terra. Why did people keep saying that? What did that mean? Of course, she was a girl. She glanced down the street, but it was remarkably empty, and the others had spanned out, blocking her path.

Joyce stepped closer. She bent down and put her face right next to Terra's. "You're going to be sooo sorry." She reached out and shoved Terra hard, on the shoulder. Terra stumbled backwards. Her heart was beating hard, and her stomach was cramped up.

"I don't think so," a voice said quietly.

Terra realized that Paula had come up behind them and stood beside her, shoulder to shoulder.

"It's nothing to do with you," Joyce frowned. "It's none of your business."

"No? Well, I'm making it my business."

Joyce scowled but hesitated. Terra wondered if everyone else could hear her heart beating.

"Seriously. If you want to beat up on Terra, you're going to have to go through me." Paula tilted her head to one side. "And Joyce, we know you don't really want to try that, do you?"

"She got me suspended!" Joyce protested.

"The way I heard it, you got yourself suspended."

"You're one to talk!" Joyce protested. "It's just luck that you haven't been suspended yourself."

Terra held her breath, but Paula only nodded. "You're probably right. But if I'd been suspended, that would have been my fault. You getting suspended is your fault. I want you to leave Terra alone. Not just now, but always."

Joyce's eyes narrowed. "And you're going to make me?"

"Yeah," said Paula calmly. "If you force me to—I'll make you."

Joyce glanced at her companions, but they seemed to shrink back a bit. She shot a malicious glance at Terra.

"Bah," grumbled Joyce. "C'mon. It's not worth it."

"You okay?" asked Paula.

Terra started breathing again. She swallowed tentatively. "Yeah. Um…hey…"

Paula looked at her.

"Uh, thank you."

"Whatever."

"Really. I mean it. I didn't think you liked me."

Paula shrugged. "You're okay."

"Oh. Well, thank you."

"Don't get a big head. It's not like I'm in love with you or anything."

Terra laughed, despite everything. "Okay. I guess I thought you were mad at me, because…"

"Because Blaine won't talk to me?" She shrugged. "That's not your fault, is it?"

Terra shook her head.

Paula nodded. "Yeah, I messed up that day. I'm really glad you stuck with her, though."

"You are?"

"Yeah. I…I do care about her, you know?"

"I believe you. Do you want me to remind her?"

Paula looked at her for a moment, then gave a short laugh. "It's like Joyce said. You really *are* a girl…"

"What?" Terra protested.

But then Paula was gone too.

*　　*　　*

At school the next day, Terra, sitting with Blaine in the cafeteria, told her about her encounter with Joyce, and about Paula's intervention.

"Huh," said Blaine. "I'm surprised she bothered to get involved; she'd usually only do that if it was something to do with her. I mean, you don't even hang out with her any more, so it's not like you getting beat up would reflect on her." She frowned and drummed her nails on the table.

127

"I think she's sorry she left you that day."

A shadow fell across Blaine's face. "Yeah, well, whatever."

*　　*　　*

"This is really fabulous," said Winter, looking at the planetary constellations that circled Terra's bedroom. "Too bad you can't submit this as some sort of science project. You'd get an 'A' for sure."

Kaitlin giggled. "Yeah, extra credit. I wonder if the science teachers make house calls."

"Hey, what's that?" she said, pointing to the blue milkbag holder on the corner of Terra's desk. It was full of pens and pencils.

"It holds milk bags."

"Milk bags?"

"Yeah, here milk comes in big plastic jugs, but in Ontario, milk comes either in cartons or plastic bags, and you put the bag in the holder."

"Oh," Kaitlin considered. "Cool."

The three girls lay horizontally on Terra's bed, staring at the ceiling and the walls around them. Their knees dangled over the edge of the bed.

"Do you think I'm a girl-girl?"

Kaitlin giggled. "As opposed to what?"

She filled them in on the previous day's events.

Winter frowned. "I'm sorry you had to take that heat by yourself. Do you think they'll come after you again?"

Terra considered. "I...I don't think so. Paula was pretty scary."

"She really is scary," Kaitlin whispered.

"Sshh," said Winter and poked her. "We're scary too, in our own way."

"So, what about this 'girl' thing? Is it insulting?"

"It's good to be a girl—so that can't be an insult," said Kaitlin.

"Yeah, but…"

Winter smiled. "Maybe they meant it as a insult, but what are they saying really? That you don't like to fight? That you're sensitive and caring?"

"Um…"

"Well, what's wrong with that…eh, girl?" Winter grinned at her.

Terra shook her head. "I guess you're right."

"Well, I usually am." Winter laughed again as Kaitlin poked her.

They lay contemplating the solar system for a while longer.

Terra cleared her throat. "Well, um…"

Kaitlin leaned over and poked her. "Out with it!" She propped herself up on one elbow. "You've been trying to tell us something all afternoon, haven't you?"

"Uh. Yeah."

"So what's up?"

"Well. I wanted to tell you that…"

Terra could feel a tight hand gripping the inside of her stomach.

"Yes?" Kaitlin raised an eyebrow.

Winter patiently stared at the ceiling.

"Just that…"

Kaitlin leaned closer. "Yes?"

In a rush of uncertainty, Terra hesitated. "Oh, never mind…"

Kaitlin grabbed a pillow and poised it threateningly over Terra's face.

Terra giggled, in spite of herself.

Winter heaved herself up to a sitting position. She pried the pillow away from Kaitlin, put it on the bed, and leaned against it. "Terra, if there's anything you want to talk about, you know that we're here to listen."

Terra nodded slowly, then she suddenly blurted it out: "I'm adopted."

The other girls looked at her for a moment, then Kaitlin exclaimed: "Hey! Me too!"

Winter poked Kaitlin gently. "Hey, this isn't about you. Not everything's about you."

Kaitlin frowned at Winter and poked her back. "I know everything isn't about me."

She turned her attention to Terra. "When were you adopted?"

"Oh, almost right away. When I was a baby."

"Ah. Do you know about your history?"

"A bit. My, uh…birthmother got pregnant, and she was just young, and things didn't work out with her boyfriend, and she put me up for adoption. That's what my parents told me."

"Wow," said Winter. "That's intense. You keep it a secret?"

"Yeah, usually. Do you think it's weird to want it to be a secret?"

"I don't know. It's nothing to be ashamed of. Are you ashamed of it?"

Terra frowned. "No. But I'm afraid people will look at me differently."

"If they do, it's their problem," said Kaitlin. "But it's a personal thing. You should talk about it, or not, depending on whether you feel like it. Sometimes I want to talk about things, and sometimes I don't."

Terra nodded slowly. "Yeah."

"But it's cool that you told us. And…" Kaitlin shot a dark look at Winter. "I *am* adopted."

Winter snorted.

"Really, I am. My stepmother Jane officially adopted me a few years ago. So now she's legally my parent, along with my dad."

"Did you want to be adopted?"

"Well…at first I wasn't sure, because I loved Mom so much, I was afraid it might be betraying her or something, even though she was dead…but I know she just wanted good things for me. And Jane, and my little sister Anna, and me and my dad—well, we're a family now, so it made sense. Ya know?"

Terra nodded.

"I know it's a lot different, though, than what happened with you. But you've got good parents, right?"

"Sure. Yeah. Most days." Terra shook her head and smiled. "No, they're good."

"Cool," said Winter. "So why are you just telling us about this now?"

"Well. I really don't think about it all that much. Well, sometimes. But not that much. It's really on my mind a lot right now though."

"Why's that?"

"Well…because she wants to meet me."

Kaitlin sat straight up. "Who does?"

"Uh…my birthmother."

They both just stared at Terra.

"Yeah," said Terra. She walked over to her dresser drawer and slowly pulled out the envelope containing the letter from Donna. She hesitated, holding it close to her chest. She pulled out the letter—and suddenly thrust it at Kaitlin, who carefully opened it, smoothing out the creases.

Kaitlin and Winter read it in silence, then sat quietly for several seconds.

"Wow. That's really something," Winter said finally.

Kaitlin nodded emphatically.

Terra showed them the photos.

"Funny-looking baby," Kaitlin mumbled, then oomphed as Winter elbowed her. "Just kidding, Terra. You were very cute."

"My head was pointy."

"Yeah," Kaitlin agreed cheerily. "I noticed."

"Um…do you think…do you think she looks like me?"

"She's got the same kind of hair. I don't know though, I honestly thought you looked a lot like your mom, when I met her."

Terra smiled. "Yeah, we get that all the time. I guess it's funny."

Winter shrugged. "My dad says people start looking alike if they live together for a long time. I don't know if it's true, but he's always saying that."

"I can see that," said Kaitlin. "Like, if everybody's eating fatty meals, maybe everyone will get chubby, or if the parents are really bad cooks, they'd all be skinny…"

"Yeah, and my mom used to cut everybody's hair the same, until we were old enough to protest about it. And she'd only dress us in her favorite colours."

"I guess that's changed, eh, Winter?" Kaitlin mused sweetly, eyeing the other girl's fluorescent yellow jumper.

Winter scowled and turned around, ignoring Kaitlin. "I think you should meet her, Terra. At least you'd know a little more then, right?"

"I guess so."

"I think it's worse not to know, than to know the truth,"

added Kaitlin. "Because our imaginations can really think up some weird things…at least mine can!"

Terra took a deep breath and admitted: "I'm really mad at her."

Winter frowned. "Why?"

"Uh…" Terra's voice dropped to a whisper. "For not wanting me."

"Yeah. It would suck to feel like that," agreed Kaitlin. "Maybe you should ask her about it."

Terra's eyes opened wide. "I wouldn't have the nerve to say that!"

Winter shrugged. "Why not? I think Kaitlin's right…for once. It's better to get real answers than to let your imagination make up all sorts of scary scenarios."

"Like monsters," interjected Kaitlin.

"What?"

"Monsters are a scary scenario. Sometimes I imagine them. Large purple monsters hiding in the closet."

"How old are you?" chided Winter.

But Terra giggled. "Not in *my* closet—have you seen how packed it is? And not under my bed, because with a captain's bed, there's drawers, and no room for monsters."

"Hey, that's cool," said Kaitlin. "You're probably safe." She paused. "Except from really tiny purple monsters."

Winter rolled her eyes. "Next thing we're going to hear Terra's having nightmares about tiny purple monsters."

Terra giggled. "Yeah. Thanks, Kaitlin."

Kaitlin tilted her wide-brimmed hat and grinned widely. "You're very welcome, my dear!"

*   *   *

That evening, Terra told her parents she was willing to meet with Donna. Even though she'd made a decision, she still felt like a heavy weight was pushing on her stomach. On Friday night, she threw up. Her mom felt her head, muttering, then made her drink flat ginger ale.

On Saturday morning, she didn't want any breakfast, but her mom cajoled her into eating a piece of dry toast and drinking some more ginger ale.

That was fairly disgusting, thought Terra. It would serve everybody right if she threw that up too.

But she didn't.

She sat by her bedroom window, waiting. At exactly ten a.m., a sporty red car pulled into the driveway. The driver sat in the vehicle for a few moments, unmoving. Then she suddenly leaped out, ran up the steps and rang the doorbell.

Terra jumped up and closed her bedroom door.

Terra could hear the murmur of adult voices. She expected someone to call her, but no one did. She could hear the voices moving, settling into the living room. She wondered if she should go downstairs too—why wasn't anyone calling her?

She sighed and lay on her bed, staring at the ceiling.

Finally, there was a light knock at the door. Her mom poked her head in. "Hi, sweetie. Donna's here. Will you come down?"

Terra got up off the bed and walked towards the door. Her mom gave her hand a quick squeeze, and they walked down the stairs into the living room.

"Donna," said her mom, "this is Terra."

The other woman, who'd been clutching a coffee cup on her lap, moved it to a coaster on the coffee table and quickly stood up. She smiled brightly at Terra and took a step towards her with her arms slightly raised, as if she was about to offer a hug.

Terra stared motionlessly at her.

The woman dropped her arms. She smiled weakly. "Hi, Terra."

"Hi."

"You can call me Donna."

Terra nodded.

"Wow. You're so big."

"I'm average-sized for my age."

"Of course…I meant, you're so much bigger than when I last saw you."

"Oh. Yeah. I grew."

Terra was surprised how small Donna was, actually— only about five feet, two inches tall. Terra already seemed to tower over her. She looked for some sort of resemblance to the image she saw every day in the mirror. But if she was expecting some sort of sense of familiarity, there wasn't one.

In fact, this Donna, with short curly hair, didn't even look much like the Donna of the photos.

"You're really beautiful, Terra."

"Oh." It's hard to be too critical of someone who's complimenting you. "Well, thank you."

Her mom nudged her. "Why don't we all sit down?"

Terra sat down in the armchair, across from Donna.

"We were just having coffee," said Donna, indicating the coffee tray.

Terra nodded. "I don't drink coffee."

"Yes, of course. That's good—you're still growing."

"Yeah, I guess so."

"Here Terra, have some ginger ale." Her mom pushed a cup into her hands. She looked down at it. At least it had bubbles. She sipped at the cool liquid.

"So you're in Grade Nine?"

"Yeah."

"Are you good at school?"

"Not too bad."

"Terra gets mostly As." It was the first thing her dad had said since Terra came into the room.

"Wow. That's good."

"Well, it's getting a bit harder, especially at the new school."

"My family moved a lot when I was a kid. My dad was in the military," said Donna.

Terra looked at her. She had no idea about this. She didn't know anything about Donna's family.

"Well, because we moved a lot, I was always going to different schools. I found that really hard." She paused. "Was it hard for you, at your new school?"

Terra looked at her parents, sitting together on the couch. She wondered if they found this as awkward as she did.

"Yeah, at first. But I'm getting used to it."

"Terra's made some nice friends," said her mom.

"Oh, that's good."

Everybody sat quietly for a few moments. Then her mother jumped up, startling Terra. "I was going to show you some albums." She pulled several photo albums out of a cupboard and placed them on Donna's lap. "There! They're mostly of Terra."

Terra craned her neck to look. She'd seen them all before, of course, but hadn't realized—yeah, they *were* mostly of her! There she was, showing off her missing front tooth, ice-skating with Mommy, fishing with Daddy. Then later, standing between her parents, smiling with Lisa, at their Grade Eight graduation.

Donna carefully turned each page, now and then exclaiming over some photo. Her eyes looked a little misty. Terra really hoped she wouldn't cry. The tightness in her own stomach had loosened up a bit, but she still felt a pressure in her head, behind her eyes.

"You're a lovely family," said Donna, quietly.

"Thank you, Donna," said Terra's mom, her hand briefly resting on that of the other woman.

"Sweetie," she said to Terra. "Why don't you take Donna for a little walk in the park? So you two can have some time to talk a bit?"

"Uh. Okay," said Terra. She stood up and put the glass of the ginger ale back on the coffee table.

She walked slowly out of the house, Donna following her, until they reached the sidewalk, where they walked side by side. A neighbour walking his dog said "Hello" cheerfully, and they both smiled and said "Hi" back.

Terra wondered what people thought, seeing them together. Did they look like they were related?

"I really like the name Terra. And how you spell it."

"Yeah. My parents liked this spelling."

"It's more unique. Do people tend to spell it wrong?"

"Oh, yeah. All the time."

Then they fell silent. "Do you have a job?"

"Oh, yes. I'm working for an insurance company. That's why I'm in town—for a conference."

"Oh."

They walked on to the little park, not far from Terra's house and sat down on one of the benches.

"This is nice."

"Yeah. There's another park near my school. It's bigger, but it's busier. A lot of the older kids hang out there."

"Oh. Well, this one is very quiet. Peaceful."

"Yeah."

"The trees are nice," Donna offered.

Terra giggled. "Yeah."

Donna pulled a small envelope out of her jacket pocket. "Listen, I brought this for you. I just jotted down a bit of a family tree, and any health information I could think of."

"Oh."

"Don't worry. Everyone's pretty healthy. I just wanted to make sure you had all the information I know."

Terra didn't know what to say about that. "So...everybody's healthy..."

"Well, my Grandma had diabetes. She died. But she was pretty old."

Terra nodded.

"I don't know a whole lot about Jack's family. But I wrote down what I know."

"Jack?"

Donna stared at her. "Jack—your, uh, birthfather. You didn't know his name?"

Terra shook her head. "Do you ever see him? Now...I mean?"

"No. Not since before you were born. No, that's not true. I saw him once after. I told him you'd been adopted."

Terra thought about that.

"What did he say?"

"I don't remember exactly. I think he was glad you were with good people."

Neither said anything for a while.

"We were too young to be parents, Terra. We were only seventeen years old."

"Yeah. That's okay. I know you didn't want me." The words were out, before Terra could stop.

"Oh, Terra."

Now tears were flowing freely down Donna's cheeks. Down Terra's too.

"It wasn't that I didn't want you—I had no idea about

how to be a parent. Yes, I felt adoption was the best thing for me; but I thought it was best for you too—to have two loving people, who were ready to be parents."

Terra nodded. She wiped her eyes with her sleeve.

"Here," said Donna and handed her a tissue.

"Thanks," said Terra, sniffing. "My mom always carries extra tissue too."

Donna smiled at her wistfully.

They didn't say anything for a few moments.

"So, um…did you have other kids?"

Donna shook her head. "No, not yet."

"Are you married?"

"No. I had boyfriends, of course, after Jack. But nothing really worked out."

"Oh."

"But," Donna smiled brightly, "I've been seeing a really nice man now, for about a year. Things are really good. We're talking about getting married."

"That's good…"

"Yeah, it really is. How about you? Do you have a boyfriend?"

Terra blushed.

"You do, don't you?"

"I don't know. He's a friend…Glenn…"

"That's nice, Terra." She paused. "But…don't be in too big a rush, okay?"

"Yeah." Terra hugged her arms tightly about herself, even though it was only a bit chilly.

Donna noticed the gesture. "We should probably get back."

Terra nodded. "Okay." She felt like maybe they should say something else, but she didn't know what else to say.

They walked slowly back to the house. "I'm glad we got to see each other—to meet again."

"Yeah."

"I'll write you a long letter at Christmas, okay?"

"Okay," said Terra. "I'll write you one too."

"Will you really?"

"Yeah."

"I'd really like that." Donna smiled.

Terra couldn't help herself. She smiled back.

"I was really nervous about coming to see you, Terra," Donna confided, almost apologetically. "I thought I was going to throw up—I have a nervous stomach."

Terra gasped aloud. "You do?"

"Yeah. I know it sounds bizarre. But I get sick to my stomach if I'm nervous."

* * *

Back at the house, Terra's dad shook hands with Donna, but to Terra's surprise, her mom gave Donna a warm hug.

Donna turned to Terra. "Um…okay. Ah, goodbye, Terra."

Terra stood awkwardly. "Bye…"

"Do you mind if I hug you goodbye?" Donna almost whispered the request.

Terra shook her head. "That would be okay."

Donna stepped forward quickly, reminding Terra how short she was. She wrapped her arms tightly around Terra and held her, just for an instant. Then she let go and stepped back. "Bye!" she called and dashed into her car. She waved, backing out of the driveway and drove off down the street.

"Well," said Terra's dad. He looked at Terra and her mom, then went back into the house.

Terra's mom's eyes were sparkling. "Are you okay, dear?"

"Yeah."

"Was that strange for you?"

"Yeah. Oh yeah." She glanced curiously at her mother. "Was it strange for you too?"

Her mom smiled. "Yeah, a bit." She linked her arm through Terra's and drew her into the house. "I love you, Terra."

"Yeah. Well. Me too," said Terra, gruffly.

"You know, I was just thinking about when you arrived, as a tiny baby. You were such a miracle for your dad and me."

Terra felt tears prickling behind her eyelids, but she blinked really hard until the feelings went away.

Dear Diary:

It was a very strange day.

Today I met the woman who could have been my mother.

I don't know what to think about that. I don't think I'm mad at her any more. But I'm not sure what I feel.

Mom says, if I want, I can get to know Donna more in the future. It seems strange, but I think that might be a good thing.

Life is weird, isn't it?

* * *

"So...how was it?" Glenn sat beside Terra on what was quickly becoming "their" bench in the small park near her house.

"It was okay," Terra answered, finally, after a long pause to think about it. "You know, I was expecting it to be a really huge deal, and it was in a way, but in another way, it wasn't. Do you know what I mean?"

"Uh, well, not really."

"Well, it was okay, but it didn't really end up feeling like this super-significant momentous event, either."

141

"You must have had high expectations."

"Yeah, I guess I really did."

"Wow. So are you disappointed?"

Terra shook her head. "You know, not really. It was okay, it was even nice. And she's out there—my parents have her address. I feel like I'll see her again."

"Huh," said Glenn. "Are you glad you met her?"

"Yeah, I am, really. I think not knowing is probably the worst thing. You can build up strange thoughts and possibilities or whatever in your mind. Now I know she's really out there, and something of what she's like, it feels okay."

"Cool," said Glenn. He gazed out into the distant. "Hey, Terra," he said.

"Yeah?"

"I, uh...I might be moving to Edmonton."

"What!"

"My mom thinks we should live together again. She's coming to town tomorrow so we can all talk about it."

"But...what about your grandparents? They'd miss you too much!"

"Yeah," he admitted. "But, they're my grandparents. My mom is my mom...I should live with her, don't you think?"

"I don't know," Terra mumbled. She didn't want Glenn to move away.

"It's not like Edmonton is really far away; it's just a couple of hours drive. I'd still be able to visit my grandparents regularly, and my friends..." He glanced at her cautiously. "And...my girlfriend."

"Oh?" she said hesitantly, looking at him.

"Yeah, I've been thinking that you're my girlfriend. Is that okay?"

Terra felt a warm feeling rush to her cheeks. "Yeah," she

nodded. "It's okay. But...I really don't want you to leave."

He stared at the grass. "Yeah. Me neither. It kinda sucks, doesn't it?"

"Yeah," agreed Terra. She repeated, emphatically. "It sucks!"

*　　*　　*

The next afternoon, the phone rang.

"Terra?" said Glenn. "Are you busy? I mean, do you think you could come over?"

Terra couldn't figure out if he sounded happy or sad. Maybe a bit excited.

"Is your mother there?"

"Yeah, you should come meet her."

"Oh," said Terra dubiously.

"Really, it will be cool. Will you come over?"

"Yeah...sure."

"Great. I'll be watching out for you. Bye, Terra."

*　　*　　*

Terra was glad she had put on a heavier coat. The air was getting cooler. When she was almost at Glenn's house, she began to wonder if she should have changed out of her jeans, put on a skirt or something. She sighed; it was too late to go back now.

She ran up the steps to Glenn's grandparents' house and rang the doorbell. "Come in, come in," smiled Grandma Lorna.

"Hey, Terra!" greeted Glenn. He led her into the living room and introduced her to a slim brown-haired woman.

"This is Terra," he said quietly. "My girlfriend."

Terra felt, rather than saw, the smiles on the faces of

Grandma Lorna and Grandpa Bob.

"It's so nice to meet you," said Glenn's mom.

"It's nice to meet you too," repeated Terra. Unfortunately, she didn't feel that way, if it meant this woman was going to take Glenn away. But she forced a slight smile.

"So...did Glenn tell you we're going to be living together again?"

"Yes..."

"Yes, it's going to be quite a change for both of us, I think."

Terra looked at the carpet.

"It's going to be a big adjustment to live in Calgary again. But I'm looking forward to it. It's the right thing."

Terra frowned, blinked. "Pardon me?"

Glenn laughed his deep, young man's laugh. "My mom's moving here. I don't have to go to Edmonton."

Terra swallowed. "Really?"

His mom smiled gently at her. "Yes, it seems like the best decision. Glenn's in the middle of his school year, and it will be nice to be closer to my parents."

"Oh," she repeated. "That's...really good."

"Yeah," grinned Glenn, "isn't it?"

fourteen

L adies and gentlemen," Mr. Brenner's voice rang over the school PA system. "Don't forget to sign up for the Daffodil Days Tea and Bakesale, our fundraiser for the Canadian Cancer Society."

"Are you going to volunteer?" Kaitlin leaned over the desk.

Terra hesitated. "I don't really know what's involved."

"Oh, it's not hard. You just have to make something for the bakesale and volunteer to serve at the tables, to sell baking and daffodils. And then you have to buy stuff too."

"Uh…."

Kaitlin smiled sweetly. "You do know my mother died of cancer, don't you?"

"Yes, yes, I'll volunteer," Terra said hastily.

Winter groaned. "Don't let her lay a guilt trip on you, eh?"

Kaitlin ignored her and held out the sign-up sheet. "Cancer's a really terrible disease. Almost thirteen hundred Canadians die of it, every week. It's the leading cause of premature death in this country."

Terra nodded. "Yeah." She quickly scribbled down her name.

"You knew that?"

"Well, not exactly, but I know it's really bad."

Kaitlin nodded emphatically and hurried off to sign up some more kids.

"It's really bad…" Terra repeated. "That sounded lame…"

Winter laughed. "No, it is bad. But seriously, you should volunteer for stuff because you think it's important, not because you feel pressured into it."

"No, I want to." Terra hesitated. "It's hard though, it seems like there are so many diseases and charities and things to get involved with. It seems people are always phoning our house or ringing the doorbell asking for some donation or another."

"Yeah. We can't fix all the problems…" Winter hesitated, then grinned. "Not at once, anyway! But really, I think the important thing is just being willing to make a real personal effort to make things better."

"Yeah, I think so too."

"Cool! So want to help me make some posters for the Daffodil Days Tea?" Before Terra could answer, Winter was handing over some markers and paper.

"Winter, you're just as into this as Kaitlin, aren't you?" Terra laughed.

Winter grinned. "Don't you know it."

* * *

Preparing for the Daffodil Days Tea took up almost all of their spare time over the next couple of weeks. When they weren't making and hanging posters, the kids—especially Kaitlin, Winter, Terra, Tracy, Blaine, Glenn and Chuck— were busy handing out flyers throughout Inglewood.

Terra agonized over her contribution to the bakesale, since she wasn't very good at any sort of cooking. "Don't worry," said Kaitlin. "I'll help you."

True to her word, Kaitlin showed up in Terra's kitchen on the weekend. Coincidentally, Lisa was able to visit at the same time. Her family was briefly in town to visit Calgary relatives, before driving up to Edmonton to celebrate her grandmother's sixtieth birthday.

Together, the three girls made four dozen cupcakes—half chocolate and half vanilla. They decorated them with a base of white icing, then, with green and yellow icing, they painted a tiny daffodil on each cupcake. Terra's mom and dad stood around the table, exclaiming at the creations.

Terra took pity on Fred and let him lick the bowl.

"Wow, we didn't know you were a chef, Kaitlin!" exclaimed Terra's mom.

"Oh, I'm not!" Kaitlin laughed. "Anyway, the recipe is Winter's."

"Well, you're quite the artist, regardless!"

"Isn't she?" enthused Lisa. "Kaitlin's are by far the best."

"Aw," blushed Kaitlin. "Thanks." She paused. "Actually, my former neighbour taught me how to draw flowers."

"Michael?" asked Terra.

Kaitlin shook her head. "No, his mother." She looked sad for an instant, then smiled. "Actually, I got two nice letters this week—one from Michael, and one from his mother."

"That's cool."

"Yeah," she nodded, with a half-smile. "It is."

*   *   *

On the day of the tea, the turnout was impressive.

"Stupendous," said Kaitlin.

"Formidable," said Winter.

After introducing her to the whole gang, Kaitlin immediately put Lisa to work serving the customers. She didn't mind at all, and poured tea and dished out desserts enthusiastically, until her family showed up to drag her away.

Lisa hugged Terra tightly. "It was great to see you again, Terra."

"You too."

"I really like your friends, Terra. And Glenn...whoa, he's really into you, isn't he?"

Terra couldn't help blushing, especially as Lisa laughed.

Then her friend paused, and asked softly, "You're doing okay now, right?"

Terra considered. "You know, I think I am. I really am."

She hugged Lisa again, who ran off with an armful of treats for the ride home.

Terra was delighted to see Grandma Lorna and Grandpa Bob come up to her bakesale table. They told her the daffodil cupcakes looked fabulous, and they bought a full dozen of them. Grandma Lorna already had a bouquet of cut daffodils under her arm. "Aren't they lovely?"

"Yes, ma'am," Terra grinned.

"We'll have to remember which of these daffodils to eat, and which to soak in water," joked Grandpa Bob.

Terra giggled.

Then Glenn's mom pulled her aside. "Terra, it was so nice to meet you. Did you know you're the first girlfriend he ever introduced me to?"

Terra shook her head. "No...but I think he's had girlfriends before."

"I think you must be special."

Terra blushed. Glenn's mom just smiled and bought a cupcake.

Terra's parents too, were in attendance, generously buying up rather a lot of sweets, including a few cupcakes. "Well, it's only fair that we finally get to try them too," her dad told her mock-brusquely. But he was smiling.

To Terra's surprise, Fred showed up too, to take away some goodies. "Well, the house still smells of the baking," he grumbled good-naturedly. "And that dough was awfully tasty."

Fred wasn't dressed in his customary overalls; he was actually wearing a shirt and tie. "Anyhow, I figured I'd better come and say goodbye."

"What?" asked Terra. The announcement was surprisingly disconcerting. "You're not leaving?"

"Well, yeah," he scratched his head. "I'm done all the work in your house."

"But…I'm going to miss having you around!"

He grinned at her. "Well, don't you worry. Wouldn't you know, but three of your neighbours are needing some renovations. Plus, your dad is talking about wanting a shed in the backyard. So you'll still be seeing a lot of me, I guess."

Terra laughed and shook her head. "I should have known!"

Fred grinned. He bit into one of her cupcakes, moaned in exaggerated appreciation, and, with a wink, wandered off.

The biggest surprise of all was the student who showed up with brownies to sell. She stopped hesitantly in front of the table where Terra and Blaine were set up.

"Paula!" exclaimed Blaine, staring at the pan, with a frown on her face.

"Don't worry," said Paula. "They're fine."

"Are you sure?"

"Of course!" Paula protested indignantly.

Then she added, rather sheepishly. "Brownies are the

only thing I know how to make."

Blaine started laughing.

Then so did Paula.

"Come on, then," said Blaine. "Let's get you set up."

The girls worked silently for a moment, arranging the brownies for sale on little plates. "There," said Blaine. "I think that looks okay. So…" she paused, "what made you do this?"

Paula shrugged. "I don't know. You guys just seemed so into it, I thought it must be important."

"Yeah," said Blaine. "I guess it is."

"It's cool, you know," said Paula.

"What is?"

"What you're doing; straightening up, or whatever."

"Oh," was all Blaine said.

"I'm trying too, you know?"

"What?" Blaine frowned slightly. "I mean, you are?"

"Yeah, well, it was pretty scary after Pete was arrested. I mean, I don't want to go there, you know? Or…" she paused and glanced at Blaine.

"Or into the hospital, like me?" Blaine filled in.

"Yeah," said Paula sheepishly. "That too."

"Really?"

"Heh. I'm giving it a try."

Blaine looked at the floor, then off in the distance, and then at Paula. "I'm…glad to hear it. Maybe we can…give it a try together.

Paula shrugged and rearranged the paper plates on her table. "Whatever."

But she had a huge smile on her face.

Terra, standing beside them, felt tears prickling at her eyes.

Blaine noticed, of course. "You're such a girl," she whispered.

With Glenn beside her, she felt tired but happy on the way home from the sale.

The air was cool and brisk, a perfect late autumn day.

"So I heard we raised two thousand dollars for cancer research," said Terra. "That's pretty good, isn't it?"

"Yeah, it sure is."

She frowned. "But even that much money won't go very far for research, will it?"

"Well, they say every bit helps. Plus, it got people thinking about cancer, and that's a good thing."

"Yeah."

"So…you want to go for a walk in the park?"

"Yeah, sure." They walked into the small park close to Terra's house. The grass was stiff and yellow, and most of the trees had lost their leaves. Terra crunched through a pile.

Glenn chuckled. "You're such a kid."

"Am not!" she protested. Grinning, she kicked at the leaves in her path.

Two little boys were tossing a big yellow ball around. One missed, and it came straight for Glenn, who kicked it back to them.

Enthusiastically, they included Glenn and Terra in their game. Terra managed to kick Glenn in the shin, much to his amusement and her embarrassment.

Then the boys' mother called, and grumbling, and shouting goodbyes, the kids ran off.

Playing up his injury, Glenn mock-limped over to a bench. As Terra and Glenn sat down, she realized it was the same bench where she'd talked with Donna.

"I like this park," she confided. "It's smaller than the other one, but there are more trees here. I really like trees."

He grinned. "I'll keep that in mind."

Terra felt a little nervous, so she talked even faster. "You know, when I first moved to Alberta, I couldn't get over how big the sky seems out here."

"Oh yeah? They do call it Big Sky Country, ya know."

"Really? Well…I can see why," Terra said, very quickly. "I wasn't sure I liked it at first; it seemed almost scary. But now I like it."

"Do you?"

She nodded.

Glenn gave her a funny look, almost shy. "If I were to kiss you, would it make you throw up?"

"Oh!" Terra's heart beat very fast. "It might," she admitted.

He laughed.

"Well, I guess I'll have to take my chances." He looked at her intently, then leaned forward and kissed her, slowly, lightly on the mouth.

The whole world seemed to tilt a little, for an instant.

Glenn smiled, slightly, at her. "Do you feel like you might throw up?"

Her cheeks felt very warm, but she shook her head. "Not even a little bit."

He chuckled and got up from the bench. He reached down and pulled her to her feet.

"Come on, Terra," smiled Glenn. "Let's go for a walk."

Dear Diary:

Today was actually a very good day.
So hey—What's up with that?

Grace Casselman has written for a number of prominent newspapers and magazines, including the *National Post*, *Globe and Mail* and *Calgary Herald*. She studied at Carleton University in Ottawa, where she earned an Honours Bachelor of Journalism. She is also the author of *Knocked Off My Knees: Coping When Chronic Illness Hits Hard* (PublishAmerica, 2003) and *A Hole in the Hedge* (Napoleon, 2003), which was shortlisted for the Canadian Library Association's Children's Book of the Year and was winner of the Golden Eagle Book Award in Alberta. *A Walk in the Park* continues the story begun in that book.

Grace lives in Calgary, Alberta, with her husband and son.

Also by Grace Casselman

Shortlisted for the
Canadian Library
Association
Children's Book of
the Year Award and
winner of the
Golden Eagle
Book Award!

An expert at fierce scowls, twelve-year-old Kaitlin presents a tough face to the world, hiding her quirky, imaginative nature. Still dealing with the loss of her mother to cancer, Kaitlin is less than kindly disposed to her stepmother and her bratty half-sister. Meanwhile, Kaitlin has firmly fastened the bulk of her antagonism on her neighbour—the odious boy, Michael, her former best pal. Now she devotes much of her energy to scheming to make him as miserable as possible. But is that what she really wants? When her Dad delivers a letter written by her Mom just before her death, Kaitlin has to deal with her own grief and anger. Unexpectedly, she's able to use that letter and her own experiences to give some help and comfort to someone who really needs it. Ultimately, she's forced to make some tough decisions about revenge and forgiveness. In the face of love and loyalty, Kaitlin has to decide what's most important in life.

*ISBN 0-929141-99-7 / 224 pages / softcover / for ages 10 and up /
5 1/8" x 7 1/2" / $8.95 U.S. / $9.95 CDN*